CABIN FRIENDS

CABIN FRIENDS

The Mystery of the
Camp Candle Lake Letters

Timothy DeBernardi

CABIN FRIENDS
THE MYSTERY OF THE CAMP CANDLE LAKE LETTERS

iUniverse books may be ordered through booksellers or by contacting:

iUniverse
1663 Liberty Drive
Bloomington, IN 47403
www.iuniverse.com
1-800-Authors (1-800-288-4677)

Because of the dynamic nature of the Internet, any web addresses or links contained in
this book may have changed since publication and may no longer be valid. The views
expressed in this work are solely those of the author and do not necessarily reflect the
views of the publisher, and the publisher hereby disclaims any responsibility for them.

Any people depicted in stock imagery provided by Thinkstock are models,
and such images are being used for illustrative purposes only.
Certain stock imagery © Thinkstock.

ISBN: 978-1-4917-9716-7 (sc)
ISBN: 978-1-4917-9715-0 (e)

Library of Congress Control Number: 2016907857

Print information available on the last page.

iUniverse rev. date: 09/12/2016

DEDICATION

For *my daughter, who inspires me every day to be the best version of me I can be. She appreciates respect and honesty, with faith.*

CONTENTS

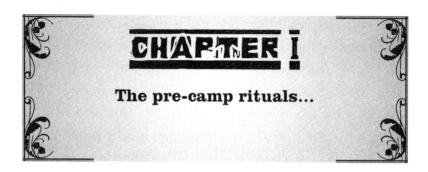

CHAPTER 1

The pre-camp rituals...

IZZIE LOOKED OUT THE WINDOW of her mother's small café. Her long curly brown hair pressed against the glass as it warmed in the sun. Her mother worked quickly in the back of the café so that they could get on their way to catch the bus for Camp Candle Lake. This was going to be Izzie's first time going to Camp Candle Lake. Looking down from the window, Izzie saw the camp checklist on her table and was quickly reminded of the school study checklists she would make. She was easily the smartest kid in her class... school... probably the country. Her school participates in the annual Academic Olympics which has five events. She won Mathletes and received a first place ribbon. Izzie went on to win four more first place ribbons that day. She was really smart. She was really funny. And, she was really caring. She didn't know Lillian, Allie, and Joe. All she knew was what was written on the letter she received from the camp. It stated that she was assigned to Cabin 29 and listed the first names of the other campers in her cabin. Soon, Camp Candle Lake would thrust the four girls into the same cabin and a world of adventure that none of them ever expected to share.

Lillian faced out the window of her parent's minivan. Her long blond hair pressed against the glass as it warmed in the sun. Her parents quietly talked about parental things in the front of the minivan while her little brother played video games on his DS. This was going to be Lillian's third time going to Camp Candle Lake. Putting her head down from the window, Lillian touched the bruise on her knee. It happened at the June school track meet. She won easily, but was accidently tripped by another student on her way to get her ribbon. She had fallen to the ground and skinned her knee and elbow. Even with a badly scraped knee, Lillian went on to win four more first place ribbons that day. She was really fast. She was really strong. And, she was a natural leader. Lillian and Allie were the best of friends at camp and shared Cabin 29 last year, with Joe and Alex. All of those girls would be life-long friends of Lillian, but clearly Allie and Lillian shared the special bond that best friends share. They were constantly on each other's arm and relied on each other all the time.

Allie looked out the window of her mom's little car. Her long red hair pressed against the glass as it warmed in the sun. Her mom quietly listened about parental things on the radio in the front of the little car, while her little sister played video games on her DS. This was going to be Allie's third time going to Camp Candle Lake. Looking down from the window, Allie looked at her new shoes, smiled and moved her feet to allow the sun to catch the sparkles on them. She got them on a shopping trip in June. When she has a good report card, her mother rewards her with a shopping excursion. Allie went on to buy four more pairs of shoes that day. She was a really good shopper. She was really fashionable. And, she was really generous. Allie recently sent Lillian a voice message telling her how much she was looking forward to seeing her at camp. Joe and Lillian would be life-long friends of Allie, but clearly Allie and Lillian shared the special bond that best friends share.

Joe looked out the window of her grandfather's pickup truck. Her short black hair pressed against the glass as it warmed in the sun. Her older brother and grandfather quietly talked about sports things in the front of the pickup, while her other older brother played video games on his DS. This was going to be Joe's third time going to Camp Candle Lake. Looking down from the window, Joe looked at her pants where there was a grease stain on her knee which happened while she was on a take-your-child-to-work day in June. She went to her granddaddy's garage, and spilled some oil on her clothes by accident while she was reaching for a wrench to fix a car. Even with a stain on the knee of her pants, Joe went on to fix four more cars that day. She was really good at fixing things. She was really tough. And, she was really sweet (on the inside). Alex, Joe's closest friend at camp, was not returning this year. Someone new would be taking Alex's bunk. Joe received a letter from Camp Candle Lake that Allie and Lillian were both returning, along with a new girl Izzie, to be in Cabin 29 with her. Allie and Lillian would be life-long friends of Joe, but clearly Allie and Lillian shared the special bond that best friends share. Joe sighed and continued looking out the window with a look of uneasiness about her. It was definitely not the traditional look that a tween should have when leaving for an awesome camp experience.

The boys were busy getting ready too. Lucas said goodbye to his mother and father as he got on his bike and headed for Camp Candle Lake. Lucas lived only a few minutes away from the camp so it was easy to ride his bike there. Lucas must have told his mother a hundred times that morning about how excited he was about everything in camp especially about seeing his best friend Eliot. This was going to be Lucas' fourth time at Camp Candle Lake. His helmet was loose and that prompted a stern warning from his mother, who always watched him ride off to camp. Lucas was athletic, funny, and had a very infectious laugh.

Eliot, on the other hand, was a total computer nut. He gave his mom grief about going to camp because it meant leaving his screen devices behind. This year, however, he had a plan. His new tablet would easily fit in the inside pouch of his suitcase. This would go unnoticed by his mom who packed everything, even his underwear. The charger would present a greater challenge for Eliot. This would have to be smuggled in the middle of a pair of his socks. He chose the wool socks, warm and practical for camp, but large enough to hide the bulky plug and cord. It worked and Eliot smiled as if he couldn't wait to show Lucas all the new games he found online.

Almost simultaneously, the parents and campers seemed to arrive at Camp Candle Lake. The huge sign was a familiar site, to most, and everyone enjoyed the smells from the opening ceremonial campfire located at the entrance to the camp. The campers gave hugs and kisses to parents, some more reluctant than others, and parted ways. Then the campers followed the instructions of counsellors and the camp owner, Frank 'Fred' Jones.

Fred was a former football player and used to be involved in many interesting life-changing events before using his family inheritance to buy Camp Candle Lake. Izzie was a little overwhelmed as this was her first time being at the camp. What seemed to be routine for everyone else was awkward and uncomfortable for Izzie. There were lots of counsellors that were there to help, but most of them were too busy catching up with each other or setting things up for upcoming events that Izzie was a little neglected. Fred, noticing this, took care of Izzie and helped her out by giving her a camp map, helping her pick out her activity sessions, and by just being nice. Fred was about to address all the new campers and showed Izzie where she could go close to the fire so she could listen to his instructions. Izzie started to feel a little more at ease. She looked around at the very active camp. Everyone who worked there was busy helping the returning campers to find their cabins, pick their activity sessions, and settle in. Everyone except the cook, Mrs. Mendax.

Mrs. Mendax was busy getting the food order from the local farmer, Mr. Perdas. Mr. Perdas, who everyone called *Big P*, owned the land next to the camp. He grew crops for the whole town and had lots of livestock. The farm supplied the camp with lots of fresh food, but it also supplied a very raunchy smell when it was time to fertilize the crops and spread manure. Big P is always heard talking about his big plans for his farm and how he longs to be more than just a local grower. He is often heard bragging to Mrs. Mendax about his plans. Most think that it is to win her affections. Eliot often jokes in front of the other campers how if Mr. Perdas were to marry Mrs. Mendax, he would be Big P and she would be Bigger P. It may seem cruel on his part, making fun of Mrs. Mendax's size, and had she been a pleasant woman, the kids would have quickly corrected him. But, seeing as she was never pleasant and only smiled when she saw disappointed looks on children's faces, even Fred chuckled at Eliot's remarks. No one appreciates the humor of the campers more than Vern Genus, the camp groundskeeper.

Vern was older, with a kind smile and hardened hands from the years of working tough jobs. There were rumors that Old Man Vern had served in the military and fought in some wars, but you would never know it from his quiet voice and his honest eyes. When you looked at Vern, you could see behind his eyes. There was a pain there that made you feel instantly sorry for him. He quietly went about his job keeping the camp impeccably clean. This was particularly noticeable in the washrooms and showers. Most camp bathrooms ended up being part of scary fire-side camp stories. They were gross, but Vern took pride in his work and made sure that each stall was hotel-quality clean.

At the gathering by the welcome fire, Fred spoke to all the new campers using a loud speaker. Izzie listened intently as he shouted out all sorts of rules and expectations. She was a little nervous that she might not remember them all. Even though she was the smartest person at the camp, she lacked confidence in social situations like this. The new campers were all told to never make a mess that they themselves were not willing to clean, because if they were caught making a mess, they just may have to clean it up. This made some of the boys look at each other with a nervous look. Izzie wasn't worried about making a mess. Her nervous look was for other reasons. As Fred's loud muffled voice belted out instructions, Izzie's tummy would not stop quivering. She felt hot and cold at the same time and her heart sank when the new campers were told it was time to report to their cabins. She had images of embarrassing herself and not being accepted race through her mind. She looked down in her lap where she was seated and there was the map showing Izzie how to get to her cabin…Cabin 29.

CHAPTER II

Meet and greet in Cabin 29...

WELL, THIS WAS IT. IZZIE was at the door. Her hands were damp and clammy and she felt strange inside. She took a deep breath and went forward through the door. She stopped immediately on the other side. She looked around and realized that there were many sets of eyes looking down at her. Everyone was staring at her except one girl who seemed to just stare at the ceiling in a nonthreatening way. Izzie felt small and vulnerable. Then she saw a smile. In an instant she was greeted by the person attached to that smile, Allie.

"I love your shoes," Allie greeted her in an awkward voice.

"Thank you," replied Izzie trying to assess the situation. Her intelligence in books was not paying off for this new social situation. "My name is Izzie." She thought telling everyone her name was the next logical social interaction.

"You're short." Lillian didn't make eye contact but must've been able to tell from where Izzie's voice came from that she was much shorter than the other girls. "How old are you?"

"I'm eleven. What's your name?"

"Are you talking to me?" Lillian asked, but not in a snotty or mean way. When no one else said anything, Lillian quickly followed with "Lillian. I'm eleven too. Where are you from?"

"I'm from Milltown, just outside of Chesterton."

"Well Izzie from Milltown just outside of Chesterton, welcome to Cabin 29. Find a bunk and settle in."

Joe just watched Izzie and didn't say a word.

Izzie made her way to a bunk closest to the door. She grabbed a hold of her bunk and pulled herself up onto the mattress and reaching down took her backpack and quietly started unpacking.

"Do you need any help?" asked Allie with a smile. She had a nice smile. She was very pretty and Izzie felt very comfortable around her immediately.

"Oh, no thank you," replied Izzie.

"I'm Allie, and the girl who is staring at you is Joe. We're all eleven." She paused for a moment, looked over at Joe, leaned in to Izzie's ear and whispered, but loudly enough for everyone to hear, "Joe doesn't shine to people when she first meets them. Don't worry, she'll come around."

"You guys already know each other?" Izzie asked.

"Yup," replied Lillian. "We have all been here before. Cabin 29 rules. Alexandra didn't come back this year. She moved and CCL…"

Izzie interrupted, "CCL?"

"Camp Candle Lake," Lillian went on while she unpacked and never did make eye contact with Izzie, "so, she moved and CCL is just too far to come now. So, I guess you're our fourth."

"She is not!" Joe erupted, "That was Alex's bed and you shouldn't be here!"

"Joe STOP!" demanded Lillian.

Allie, who was unpacking her beautiful camp wear, looked up and saw the commotion.

"She is not Alex. Alex should be here. Alex was my friend. That was Alex's bed!" Joe continued.

Izzie felt threatened and scared.

"Joe!" Lillian demanded her attention again. "It is not Izzie's fault that Alex couldn't come. You can't be mad at her."

Joe, with sadness and anger in her eyes finally looked at Lillian.

Lillian motioned for Joe to calm down and there was a moment of silence.

Allie broke the silence "Izzie, Joe can be a great friend, once she gets to know you and trust you." Izzie was not comforted by Allie's comments and looked up at Joe. An innate sense of defence came upon her. She had read about this before but never experienced it. It was fight or flight as she recalled. When faced with aggressive behavior, a person will either stay and fight or take off running in flight. Fight.

"I don't expect you and I ever to be friends, and I doubt we'll ever like each other, however we are in the same cabin and you will BACK OFF and leave me alone!"

Allie looked at Lillian, moved toward her and put her arm around the top part of Lillian's arm. Izzie was no Alex. Izzie watched as Lillian nodded a nod of reassurance to both girls and provided a look of 'I got your back Jack. *This girl maybe crazy*'. Their sisterly bond seemed to kick in as if they knew exactly what each other were thinking. Unfortunately for Izzie, she didn't have a clue what they were thinking. It was just silent again.

Allie took Joe by the shoulder and led her back to her bunk. The outburst by Izzie had worked. Joe was not a danger at present. However, it also seemed to alienate the girls of Cabin 29. The silence was beginning to get awkward. BANG! The door burst open!

The silence was broken by Eliot and Lucas who burst into the cabin laughing.

"Eliot! Lucas! What if we were changing?" exclaimed Allie. "You guys are jerks!"

Then the girls, all but Izzie, laughed. The boys joined in the laughter and there were hugs and greetings all around.

"You're lucky Heather wasn't here. You'd both be going home the first day you got here," said Lillian.

"Or worse…" said Allie.

Leading Eliot to say, "Like doing kitchen duty with Old Lady Mendax!"

"Ewww" said Lucas. "I hate dishes"

"I hate Mendax," Eliot chimed in snidely.

"Hey, be nice," said Lucas. "Who are you?" he said with a smile to Izzie.

"Izzie," was all she could say staring at Lucas with a strange new feeling in her tummy. The feeling seemed to travel from her tummy all the way up to her head and she felt light-headed. She was smitten.

Everyone just sort of looked toward Izzie with silence. Joe moved between Lucas and Izzie. "Did you try the newest 'Bangle Blast' game yet?" Joe asked Lucas, but Eliot jumped in and replied.

"Yes! And I brought the new 'Drop Beat' game on my tablet."

"Dude! You snuck electronics here?" inquired Lucas.

"Yes! I can't be unplugged all camp. I have needs."

Everyone chuckled and Lillian chimed in, "You need to leave before Heather gets here and you guys get into trouble."

Lucas agreed and took Eliot's shoulders in his hands, turned him around and walked him out the door. He paused for a second, leaned back, looked at Izzie and said "Nice to meet you," and with that they were gone. Izzie smiled and sighed. Her eyes focused on the door where Lucas had just passed through. Izzie cleared her head, gave it a shake, looked up and saw Joe staring across at her. Joe was not smiling.

Izzie tried to ignore Joe and just went about her business unpacking. She couldn't believe all the clothes Allie was unpacking. She had a ton of outfits and accessories. Izzie noticed these little bows that Allie had for her hair and thought they looked awesome and it appeared that Allie had enough for each day she would be at camp. She couldn't help but feel the weight of Joe's stare. Even when she couldn't see Joe, Izzie knew she was still staring at her. Just when Izzie thought Joe might actually try to hurt her, Heather came in and broke the tension.

"Hello campers!" said Heather with a great big smile. She was beautiful and much older. She must have been at least 18 years old. She was well put together and looked exactly like a camp counsellor out of a camp brochure. Izzie had never seen such a beautiful woman and hoped one day she could smile like that. Heather was clearly one of those people that everyone liked and wanted to be like.

"Cabin 29, my favourite cabin, are you guys ready for an awesome month?"

The girls all went and hugged her. "Hi Allie," she said as they did some sort of secret hand shake, "How are you? It is so good to see you again!" She saw Lillian and took her hand and pulled her back and said "Lillian, look how tall you are and I love your hair. Did you get your ears pierced? You're so grown up and it's only been a year. Allie," she said pointing at her shoes, "I have to get a pair of those. Those are awesome. And my Joe, it's so good to see you again!" Joe was finally smiling with delight and Izzie felt a little more at ease.

"And you must be Izabella."

"Izzie, please."

"Well Izzie, it is nice to meet you. Have you met everyone in Cabin 29 so far?"

"Yes."

Heather, as if sensing some tension, said "Well, nothing brings the crew together better than all of us surviving Mrs. Mendax's opening meal."

The girls all laughed. All but Izzie. Heather stood at the door and instructed the girls of Cabin 29 to go to the mess hall where dinner would be served. Izzie wasn't quite ready. Heather looked back at her and smiled. It was a smile of reassurance and hope. Izzie felt comfortable and knew that she was going to enjoy the camp eventually. She was optimistic that dinner would change things for the better.

"Do you need help?" asked Heather.

"No, I'll be there in just a minute."

"Okay, well if you get lost, follow the signs with the purple circles to the mess hall. If I don't see you in five minutes, I'll come get you. Okay?"

"Thank you. That's nice of you."

And with that, Izzie was alone in Cabin 29. After attending to a few final details before getting ready, Izzie left the cabin. She followed the purple circles to the mess hall. Just as she was coming to the side door of the mess hall, the one she could get in the easiest, she saw a large lady with no smile talking to a large man unloading a truck of its contents. They seemed to be having a disagreement of some sort. The lady was miserable and the man seemed to just laugh her off as if what she was saying meant little to him.

Heather was right. Dinner was a lot of fun. The girls all sat together and by the time Izzie got there, Heather had all the girls in a friendly comfortable mood. They even left a space for Izzie to join them easily.

"Pull up here Izzie," Heather said.

"Thanks," Izzie settled in and tried to make herself comfortable.

"You only missed Fred telling everyone about the cheer contest."

"What's that?" asked Izzie.

"It's something we win every year and the winner doesn't have to do kitchen duty once the entire time at camp," Lillian said.

"And we win every year," Allie said, "but we'll need your help to be really loud."

Izzie whispered, "I can be loud."

Everyone laughed at how quiet Izzie said she could be loud. Izzie laughed too. Everyone from Cabin 29 taught Izzie the cabin cheer. Each cabin in the mess hall had to participate and the team that was voted the worst cheer had to do kitchen duty that night, clearing and cleaning all the dishes after dinner. Cabin 29 had won every year and Izzie didn't want to let them down. This was her chance to really make an effort to fit in with the other girls. She felt insecure but, just like she didn't let Joe intimidate her earlier, she wasn't going to let this intimidate her either. Izzie could tell that Joe was also starting to accept Izzie as the newest addition to her cabin.

"We always start with one person leading and the others join in. Lillian usually leads," Joe instructed Izzie.

"Okay, what do I do?" said Izzie.

The girls taught Izzie the cheer and after hearing some of the other cheers Izzie gained even more confidence. She knew for a fact that the cheer the girls taught her was not going to be the worst cheer. One cheer was just 'We're weird'. It was Izzie's group's turn and she waited for Lillian's cue and then belted out at the top of her lungs,

We are the cabin
that makes
Cabin friends so great
We are the cabin
that makes
Cabin friends so great
Cabin 29
is so fine
we are friends
'til the end of time.

This was the winning cheer, three year's running; make that four. The girls won again and Joe high-fived Izzie. They bonded over dinner.

After dinner, as they followed the path back to their cabin, the entire camp was filled with their laughter and joy. They moved along quickly so they could get ready for the campfire. Lillian held the path rope all the way up the door and was the last to stop laughing.

"What is it?" she asked.

"The letter on the door," Allie said.

"That's not normal," said Joe.

It was stuck to the door with a large dirty nail and on the envelope it said "GET OUT!"

CHAPTER III

Let her find the letter...

THE GIRLS STOOD STARING AT the letter. All but Lillian who anxiously reached around putting her hand on the door right next to the letter, grazing it slightly with the side of her forearm. She grabbed it, and ripping it down, she handed it over to the girls. Allie took it from her and opened it. The letter inside was written in shaky dark ink. It simply reiterated what the envelope said. In large letters it said "Get out!"

"Is this supposed to scare us?" Lillian asked after Allie read it aloud. "I bet it was Eliot."

"I don't think so," Joe said looking down at Izzie.

"What?" said Izzie, "It wasn't me."

"Sure," said Joe in a very sarcastic way.

"I swear," Izzie said. Allie looked at Joe. Joe looked back. Izzie felt like both girls seemed very suspicious of her.

"Come on, seriously. Why would I try and scare you guys? Remember, '*We are the cabin, that makes...*'" But she was quickly cut off.

"Because you don't like me," Joe said.

"I admit that you and I didn't have a great start, but I would not do something like this."

Lillian felt the nail in the door with her fingers. "Guys, where would she get a nail?"

"But she was so late coming to the mess hall," Joe said staring down at Izzie.

"But the nail is so high up and she is… short. She would have to jump and nail at the same time."

"That does seem impossible Joe?" Allie said.

Izzie could see that Joe was processing it and didn't know what response to anticipate.

"I guess it's not possible," Joe said slowly.

"It was probably an Eliot prank," said Allie.

Izzie exhaled with relief.

"Izzie, can you forget how these guys lost their heads for a minute? We have got to get a move on to get to the campfire," Lillian said.

"Okay," Izzie breathed another sigh of relief. As she went into the cabin and got ready for camp circle Izzie felt uneasy.

"Ya, lets plan to get Eliot back!" laughed Allie.

Izzie noticed that Joe watched every move she made for the rest of the night, and not in a good way.

The next morning Izzie woke up. She was staring up at the bunk above her. On the wood that held Allie's mattress on the top bunk was written in marker 'Cabin 29 Rulez'. It was signed by Allie, Lillian, Alex and Joe. Izzie wanted to add her name but knew that she didn't fit in, at least not with Joe yet. She looked around and was rather startled to see Joe's bed across from her was empty.

The camp was quiet and a blueish morning light peeked through the cabin window curtain, causing strange shadows to form. Izzie took a moment to admire her surroundings. The smell of the wood constructed cabin, with the log style bunks, blended in a sweet way with the morning cool air. Plaid blankets draped from the corners of the upper bunks and the sounds of slumber came from where Allie and Lillian were fast asleep. Allie mentioned three times the previous night that she definitely was not a morning person. A beam of light from the rising sun revealed a trail of cabin dust that danced in the air all the way to Lillian's face. It didn't seem to bother Lillian as she appeared to be in a deep sleep. Izzie took a cleansing breath and there was a hint of campfire in the air, perhaps from Mrs. Mendax preparing breakfast for the over two-hundred campers and staff who would awake with eager tummies. The thought of last night's letter incident seemed long ago.

The previous night's festivities and the morning peacefulness seemed to make Izzie forget the awful start she had at the camp. Soon, Heather would be in to wake the remaining girls and go through morning routines before breakfast. There would be a reading of the camp credo, the raising of the flag, and the march to the mess hall. The campers and camp counsellors would all gather at the centre of the camp with the owner of the camp, Frank, who everyone called Fred. At least, that is what Heather told Izzie would happen during last night's campfire. Izzie had listened intently while crushing three s'mores. But the feeling of joy from last night quickly faded from Izzie's mind as a flash at the way Joe had stared at her all night; her eyes trying to figure Izzie out. Joe! Where was Joe?

Izzie quietly pulled herself out of the bottom bunk. She sat down and pulled a hoodie on as the cool air felt colder when she wasn't wrapped up in her blankets. She made her way to the door of the cabin moving slowly and looking up at the top bunks where Allie and Lillian lay motionless. With the cabin door now open, Izzie looked around for Joe. She moved forward just outside the cabin entrance and looked from side to side. There was no one around. The camp stood still like a painting. The leaves on the trees were still and quiet. Then Izzie heard the cracking of dry sticks and crunching of leaves underfoot as someone, or something, hustled by and startled Izzie. Tempted by curiosity, Izzie moved toward the edge of the forest to see what made the noise.

A shadow of a figure moved quickly in the trees but the morning light and the shadows from the forest made it difficult for Izzie to see who or what it was. Izzie found a flat path and went closer, trying to keep her intellectual perspective, mainly knowing she is smart enough to know that it wasn't a monster and probably just Joe running and trying to scare her. She moved as fast as she could navigating quickly but carefully not to hit a root or a stone that may throw her off course and send her tumbling into the woods and off the path. As she made her way through the forest she realized whoever, or whatever, had long since lost her. She stopped. Birds made sounds in the trees. Sounds Izzie was very unfamiliar with; creepy, but beautiful sounds. Then Izzie heard a more familiar sound. It was the sound of water. The sound of water cascading and falling drew Izzie to move toward it.

Then a horrible sound pierced through the noises of the water.

"HELP!" A cry came from close to the water. The sound was sheer panic and deep life-threatening fear. "Help! Help! Help!" The more Izzie heard the cries for help, the more terror she felt. She moved toward the sounds. The cries of terror were starting to be muffled with the sound of crying. The voice begged for help as if pleading for its life. Izzie saw a hand clutching a rock, another clutching a root and arms that disappeared off the edge of a cliff.

Izzie fell flat on the ground and maneuvered closer to the hands and yelled "I'm here, I'm here!"

Izzie quickly calculated that the bank of the river went down five or six feet. The river moved very quickly and would be a challenge for even the most skilled swimmer, something Izzie was not. The rocks in the white waters would prove to be dangerous to any skilled canoers and deadly to swimmers. The waters raged and didn't stop until much further down the river. In the distance, Izzie could see a farm, probably Big P's farm, where the waters finally slowed and meandered their way into a large pond. If Izzie couldn't help the person hanging on for life, Mr. Perdas might have something very disturbing end up on the shores of his farm.

Izzie slid forward. She could feel the cold mud of the bank on her tummy and elbows as she reached for the hands. She strained forward and with a single thrust grabbed a hold of the wrists of the person hanging. "Can you get your foot on a rock or something to push yourself when I pull?" shouted Izzie.

"I think so!" shouted a voice. Izzie found it hard to hear with the sound of the water rushing.

"I'll count to three… one…two…three!" and with that Izzie pulled with all of her arm muscles and arched her back to add more leverage. The arms came forward and a pile of tween landed part on top but mostly next to Izzie. It was Joe.

The two laid gasping for breath. They didn't say a word for several minutes and then Joe started laughing. Izzie, too, found herself laughing and trembling from fear. Joe helped Izzie up and the two of them brushed as much mud from each other's clothes as possible. "Thank you," Joe said. Her eyes were kind and you could tell that she was sorry for the mistrust she had in Izzie. "I know it wasn't you that put that letter there. I also know that it wasn't you that made Alex not come back."

"It's okay," said Izzie as she turned to head back to camp. Joe walked beside her except where the trail was bumpy. Joe would walk behind Izzie then. "What were you doing near the water? Why did you run away from me this morning?"

"I didn't run from you. I was running after whoever put the letter on our cabin door. I heard a knock this morning and it woke me up. I peeked out the window and saw that cabin 27 had a letter on their door. I went over and got it and when I was on my way back to our cabin to show you guys I heard someone in the woods. When I walked closer I didn't hear anything. Then I heard our cabin door open and before I could ask for help I saw the figure of a person run toward the river."

"You could have been killed Joe!"

"I didn't think it was anything serious, just Eliot playing tricks on us! But as I got close to the water, I realized I had lost whoever it was and that's when I slipped."

Izzie inquired, "You sure you weren't pushed?"

"Ya. I just slipped on the wet mud," replied Joe sheepishly, "I feel stupid."

"Don't ever say that Joe. You're not stupid," defended Izzie.

"Thanks. But please don't tell anyone Izzie. Please!"

"Lillian and Allie will have to know. After all, isn't being part of Cabin 29 being able to trust your cabin mates?"

They smiled at each other and made their way back to the cabin. When they opened the door, they were greeted by Allie and Lillian and told them the entire story.

"Do you still have the letter from 27?" asked Lillian.

"In my pocket, but it is a little damp," said Joe.

"Hand it to Izzie. Izzie read it to us," Lillian ordered.

"GET OUT, OR GET HURT."

CHAPTER IV

Do the Dew...

"HEY LUCAS."

"Ya, Eliot?"

"What kind of camper is above all other campers?"

"I dunno."

"A pop-up camper."

Lucas didn't laugh. Eliot was always telling horrible jokes like that. Sometimes he read them on the internet and other times he made them up. Neither were good. The two kept reading their comics laying on their respective bunks. Lucas always slept on the top bunk as Eliot, in the past, once woke Lucas up with a dripping mattress. The story of how Lucas flipped out when it happened has quickly grown to be a camp legend.

They would have been about seven at that time. Lucas laid in the bottom bunk. Eliot, being addicted to Mountain Dew ever since the company's letter contest, always had a can in bed with him to drink before falling into a deep sleep. Drinking all that soda was not healthy, nor was it good on the bladder before sleep time. The letter contest by Mountain Dew was a huge success. At the bottom of each can was a letter. If you could spell certain words properly, you would win that prize. For example, the first year, Eliot collected the letters, B, I, K, E and won a BMX bike. His parents had to pay shipping and taxes so it wasn't totally free and the bike was too big for Eliot at the time, but Eliot told Lucas that he was hooked on that winning feeling. So much so, that he probably paid for that bike ten times with the amount he spent on Mountain Dew. It was shocking that with consuming so much soda, that Eliot was slender and never had a cavity. He did have one small problem though, as Lucas had discovered years ago.

Drip. Drip. Drip. Lucas was a seven year old sleeping soundly under his new bunk mate, Eliot, when he felt the first splash of what he thought was water dripping on his forehead. Then it happened. As Lucas lay there, too tired to move, and not awake enough yet to fully comprehend what was happening, the drip that plunged to his forehead made a wet trail down his cheek. And, like a canoer meandering and navigating the path of the river rapids, the liquid banked right toward Lucas' mouth. With his lips slightly parted, it entered through the corner of his mouth and dripped along his tongue into the back of his throat. He jumped up at the unfamiliar taste and smacked his head on the bunk above him. The pain was intense and he stumbled to hop out of bed where he smacked his head again, this time on the ladder that went to the top bunk. Coughing and gagging Lucas freaked out and woke the other three boys in the cabin. Eliot shone his flash light on Lucas from the top bunk.

"What is going on?" asked one of the other boys in the cabin.

"Ya, Lucas, what's wrong with you?"

"You pee'd the bed and it's all over me… it went in my MOUTH!" gagged Lucas now scrambling to look for water as the flashlights of the other boys moved frantically around the cabin like prison guards looking for a convict trying to escape in the night.

"Lucas," said Eliot.

But Lucas kept gagging and looking for water.

"Lucas…Lucas!"

The cabin went quiet.

Eliot put the flashlight on his own face. The other boys did too.

"I didn't pee. My soda spilled."

There was silence. The boys in unison burst out laughing. Eliot cleaned up the spill as best as he could but he had to switch bunks with Lucas and four years later has yet to be given the top bunk. It was the first time that had happened and it was also the last.

Bang! Bang! Bang!

"What was that?" whispered Eliot.

"Sounds like someone is at our door," replied Lucas.

"That didn't sound like a knock," said one of the other two boys in the room, "It sounded like someone just nailed our door shut."

It was the end of day two at the camp, and other than the girls from Cabin 29 acting weird all day, the day went pretty normal.

"Should we go and check the door?" whispered Eliot.

"You guys are being silly. It was probably Allie or Joe and that new girl… Izzie, playing a joke on us. I'll look," and with that, Lucas jumped up and went for the door.

When he opened the door, which was not nailed shut, he saw nothing but a quiet campground. Holding the door open with his left hand and leaning against the cabin with his right, he gazed at the other cabins and the paths that lead to the beach, the mess hall and the camp center. His head darted to the right as he thought he saw someone duck off in the distance. He knew though, or at least he strongly felt, like his nerves just got the better of him, and he went to close the door. As he did, the moon light reflected off the nail in his door that held an envelope at eye level to Lucas.

"Holy bat turds!" said Lucas in a slow monotone voice.

"That can't be good," said Eliot who sprang from the bottom bunk.

Lucas pushed the door wider open so that the outside part of the door was far enough in that the boys could see the envelope. On the front it said, "HEED MY WARNING!"

"Get out or get hurt!" read Lucas to the other kids. They stood there with paper and envelope in hand. They were quiet.

"I think we should tell Brian," said one of the other two boys.

"Ya, we have to tell our counsellor," said the other, "but there's no way I'm going to his cabin."

"Well, I'm not going."

Lucas and Eliot were quiet and just looked at each other. Lucas wanted Eliot to use his tablet to do some research on this. Lucas earlier had told Eliot to be careful and not to take out his tablet because if one of the other two boys in his cabin told on him it would be taken away or worse, Eliot could be sent home. With the other two boys visibly shaken, Lucas decided now was the time to earn the boys' trust and get Eliot to take out his tablet. Lucas motioned for Eliot to get it.

After a ceremonial sharing of a Mountain Dew, and an oath taken by the two boys, swearing them to secrecy, Eliot took out his tablet and hacked into the camp WiFi and started searching to see if this had ever happened before. Eliot and Lucas laid next to each other and hid the light of the tablet under a blanket. The other two boys kept watch in case someone came to check on them.

The search proved futile. They searched 'Camp Scares' and all they found was a bunch of links to 'Scooby Doo' and camp stories. Nothing seemed to be on the first page of Google for anything they searched. Mind you, they never once went to the second page of Google. It seems that there could be unicorns, treasure maps, and the cure for every disease on page two of Google searches and the world would never know.

"Hey Eliot?"

"Ya, Lucas."

"Do you think 29 got one of these letters last night and that's why they were so weird today?"

"Do you think that the girls did this, and they were weird today because they were planning it?"

"No," replied Lucas. "I think they got one too. Let's ask them in the morning." Lucas pulled the covers back and Eliot closed the tablet case. "No one say anything to Brian yet, because if it was the girls, I don't want them to get into trouble."

"Ya, we could just get them back," laughed Eliot, and the boys eventually drifted off to sleep.

The next morning the boys were woken by a knock on their door. It was a soft knock, like if a knock could whisper.

CHAPTER V

The ink-stained hand...

THE GIRLS HAD WOKEN UP bright and early. Earlier than all the other campers, just in case the mystery person decided to attack their door again. The only other person up at that hour was Vern. He was tending to the grassy areas making sure that the sprinkler heads were working and the grass was getting its morning shower. Izzie and the girls of 29 got dressed quickly. Joe prepared to open the cabin door.

"Brace yourselves!" she said.

Izzie braced herself for the cold morning air that would rush into the nice warm cabin. Their cabin smelled of fresh flowers and a hint of cinnamon as all girl cabins should smell. Words cannot describe the fumes and toxins that flow through a boy's cabin by morning. In addition to the rush of cold air, Izzie and the girls also had to be ready that on the outside of their door, there could be another letter.

There wasn't a letter, but the rush of the cold air and the anticipation of the moment still lead the girls to shiver. Then they jumped and were startled. A large imposing figure stood facing them from the path outside their door. Izzie gripped

Joe's forearm. It was Vern. The girls all giggled quietly and let out a deep breath of relief and Izzie let go of Joe.

"What are you girls doing up so early? Not going to cause any mischief are you?"

"No, Mr. Genus," replied Lillian. Izzie found Vern's voice was easy to enjoy. There was something soothing and grandfatherly about it.

"Do I want to know what you guys are up to?" he said with a smile.

"No, Mr. Genus," replied Lillian again with a smile of her own and a little giggle.

As Vern told the girls of the time he snuck out of his cabin, back in the day, Allie looked down at his hands. His left hand was clean, as you might suspect in the morning, but his right hand had...

Allie gripped tightly onto Lillian's arm. Izzie knew that Allie must have just seen something or figured something out and started scanning Vern and the surrounding area. Izzie noticed that Lillian remained her normal self, with composure, which led Izzie to believe that either Lillian didn't notice the grip Allie had on her, which was unlikely, or that she was cool as ice. Izzie didn't notice anything strange behind or around Vern and just hoped that later Allie would explain why she grabbed so tightly onto Lillian's arm.

"... and that's how we got the nickname 'Marshmallow cabin'. It was right there in 27. Oh boy I tell you. I thought we were in for it." Vern paused as he looked at Allie's hands around Lillian's arm. Allie eased up on her grip a little. "Well...what's camp without a little mischief?" He scanned the girls cautiously.

Izzie sensed that he was looking for something or perhaps he suspected something or maybe he had something to hide. No matter what it was, Izzie didn't like the feeling. "Now, you girls tell me which way you were heading and I'll be sure to tell you that I'm going the opposite way." Vern finished and smiled.

All the girls but Lillian looked at each other for approval.

"Allie, point to the mess hall," directed Lillian.

"I'll be going the other way," said Vern. He tipped his hat with his ink stained hand and Izzie and Joe's eyes widened.

Once the girls were far enough down the path away from Vern, Lillian stopped the girls and said, "Okay, what is with the gasping and the gripping? You almost took my arm off back there."

"Vern had ink all over his right hand," Allie said.

"His left was perfectly clean," Izzie jumped in.

"No way! You don't think that…" Lillian was interrupted by Joe.

"Vern wrote the letters."

"Wait. Having ink on his hands does not prove that he wrote the notes. And what possible reason would he have for doing that?" Lillian asked.

The girls just stood there. Puzzled by the newest clue, Izzie tried for a moment to piece together what reason Old Man Genus would have for trying to scare the campers and ruin the camp. After coming up with nothing, Izzie snapped out of the deductive fog and woke the girls from their hazy thinking.

"Let's go!"

As the girls went down the path, Lillian motioned for them to stop and whispered "Do you guys hear that?" No one moved. A few seconds later, Izzie heard the sound of footsteps and some kind of robotic sound. The footsteps were moving quickly and lightly and as the girls held their breath and Izzie started to expect something terrible, Heather popped out and almost ran the girls over. She yelped and collapsed bending over at the waist and laughed. As she removed her headphones the robotic-like noise got louder. It was her music. Heather pressed pause to stop the music on her cellphone. She had difficulty breathing and based on the amount she glistened, she had been jogging for some time.

"This is how you keep in such good shape Heather?" Joe asked with admiration.

"Love the active wear," Allie said with admiration.

"I love that song you're listening to," Izzie said with admiration. She heard what Heather was listening to and admired her taste in music. She also heard the other two compliments and picked up on the social cue that she too should say something nice.

Before Heather could reply to the barrage of compliments Lillian asked, "What smells?"

Heather laughed. "That would be me Lillian. When you jog, you sweat. When you sweat, you stink. Don't worry, I'll hit the showers before breakfast."

"Oh my goodness Heather, I didn't mean to …"

"Don't worry about it Lillian," laughed Heather, "What are you guys doing out of your cabin so early?"

"Well…" started Allie.

"We were going to offer to help out Mrs. Mendax," Izzie jumped in and cut off Allie. "We figured if we offer to help make breakfast it might keep us out of campfire clean up." Izzie didn't trust that Allie's response would be as simple and believable as the one she had thought up and thought it best to interrupt her and present her idea.

"You guys already are exempt from dish duty. Are you really that scared of cleaning?" Heather asked as she put on her headphones once again. Izzie clued in that she could pretty much say anything and Heather wouldn't have cared. It was obvious that Heather just wanted to get back to her exercise.

"Well there are these letters being posted on doors that say 'get out' and we saw Vern and he had ink on his hands and we think it might be him. Oh and I saved Joe's life yesterday as she chased a figure into the woods where she almost fell into the raging water that runs down to Big P's farm." Izzie pictured herself saying in a flash, but she actually said, "Well we got to keep Allie's manicure nice, ya know?"

"Okay, be good," Heather replied, and as Izzie suspected, she didn't even seem to really listen.

"Why didn't you let me tell her?" Allie asked Izzie.

"You were going to tell her the truth? I was afraid that you were going to make up a story so I interrupted. I felt a little bad doing it as I didn't want to hurt your feelings or be rude, but now I'm really glad I did. Right now, everyone is a suspect. We don't know who's doing this or why. All we know is that someone…"

"…or something." Izzie was interrupted by Joe.

They paused and looked at Joe. Izzie carried on, a little slower and a little calmer. "…is trying to scare us and get us to leave the camp."

Lillian put her hand up with a sense of urgency to quiet everyone. "Guys! I hear footsteps on the path behind us," she whispered in a panic.

Izzie and Joe moved back into the dense bush behind them and grasped at Allie and Lillian and pulled them in to hide. They were silent, trying hard to not even breathe. The footsteps walked slowly, heavy, as if the stones on the path were being punished just for being there. Izzie glided forward, silently, like a ninja, to get a better look without being seen. It was Fred, the camp owner. Izzie wanted to let out a sigh of relief but knew she should stay silent until he was long gone. Fred seemed tired as if he had been up all night. His footsteps in his large hiking boots seemed to make his feet heavy and difficult to move. The morning sun reflected off of his backpack buckles and the silver pen he held in his hand.

"Pen!" thought Izzie. She screamed in her head so loud, but never made a sound on the outside. Her eyes just widened to the point where it hurt her eyelids. Then, in an instant, Fred was gone.

"It was definitely Fred, and he definitely had a pen!" Izzie whispered to the girls frantically.

"You don't mean...a real pen! Like with ink and everything. Quick call the cops and arrest him!" whispered Lillian in a very sarcastic tone. "I have a pen. Are you going to arrest me too?" Lillian reached into her pocket and pulled out a pen.

Izzie, feeling sheepish, retorted, "You have the right to remain silent, you have the right..."

The girls giggled really quietly.

"Let's just go see Lucas and Eliot," said Allie.

They all nodded in agreement and made their way to the boy's cabin, being careful not to be seen. When they approached the boy's cabin door Joe knocked on the door. It was a soft knock, like if a knock could whisper.

The door opened and the girls were standing on one side of the door looking at the boys and the boys stood looking at the girls. Both groups were holding letters in their hands.

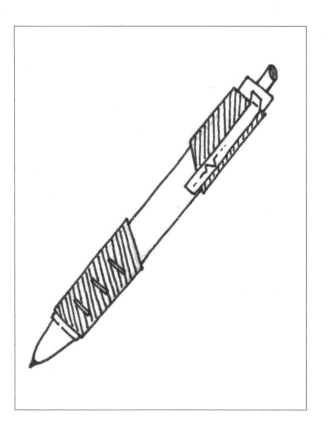

CHAPTER VI

Someone has some explaining to do...

"GET IN HERE!" LUCAS WHISPERED and the girls quickly hustled into the boy's cabin. The morning light was dimmed more in the boy's cabin because of its location deeper into the woods. There was a definite difference between the cabins, more than just the superhero sleeping bags and lighting. The wooden log bunks were the same as the girls and the boys were in one of the smaller cabins like the girls too. Most cabins had a porch and three bunk beds but these had only two bunks and no porch to climb. The floors in the boy's cabin were the same as the girl's cabin with large wood panels that seemed to be there for 100 years. They were worn, faded, smooth, and showed their age when they were walked on. Each step was a hollow drum sound with a matching creepy creak. Yes, the cabins were a lot alike, but there were differences. One Lillian pointed out in a violent whisper.

"Oh my goodness it wreaks in here!" Lillian waved her hand in front of her as if moving the air around might cause it to smell better. It didn't.

"Ya that was mostly Eliot" said Lucas.

"Ya....sorry about that," Eliot said quietly. "But really we can blame Mendax. She makes the food that changes into the methane gasses found deep within my underbelly."

"Enough!" said Lillian. "The faster we figure this out, the faster I get out of this gas factory."

"I think my clothes are wilting." Allie said staring down at her outfit.

"Just a good excuse to go shopping again." Izzie chimed in trying to put a positive spin on a very smelly situation. She felt queasy from the smell.

Allie's disgusted face staring down at her outfit changed to a large smile. Her eyes didn't move though, just her mouth smiled. Izzie was careful not to open her mouth more than necessary as this smell was one thing she didn't want to change into a taste. Izzie took all the letters and examined them carefully in her lap. She looked at one and then the other two. Lucas looked over her shoulder. She examined the first one found on Cabin 29, then the second one Joe found on Cabin 27 and then the third one that the boys had found.

"Report," said Lillian in a tone that was pleasant but full of leadership.

"They're all definitely written by the same person with the same pen," reported Izzie.

"But why?" asked Lillian.

"I don't know but I think we should start asking some questions and get to the bottom of this," Lucas said.

"I think we should tell Heather," Allie said.

"Heather. I'll tell Heather. I'll go see Heather, if that's who you want to tell, and by who I mean Heather, and by Heather..." rambled Eliot. Izzie was admittedly not that socially adept but even she could tell that Eliot could not contain his crush. When all eyes were staring at him, in a look of disapproval, he leaned back against a bunk post and said, "… it's cool. Whatever. Just if you need someone to tell her or whatever. Just sayin. It's cool." His voice drifted quieter as he rambled.

"Smooth," said Lucas.

"No. We can't trust anyone until we get some answers," Lillian said.

"We saw Fred with a pen," Joe told the boys.

"Huh?" said Lucas.

"It's cool," said Eliot, who was obviously still day dreaming about Heather.

"Ya, on our way here, we saw Fred walking really exhausted-like, and he had a pen in his hand. And before that, we saw Vern with ink all over his right hand," explained Izzie.

"Whoa," said Lucas.

"It's cool," repeated Eliot.

"Okay, I'll get Eliot down from the clouds and we'll get to work on research trying to find out why someone might do this sort of thing. He's already hacked the office Wi-Fi and so far we've come up with nothing, but we'll keep trying. You guys should split up and talk to Vern and Fred." Lucas sounded like a football coach motivating his team.

"Sounds good. Allie and I will talk with Fred. Joe, you and Izzie go talk to Vern and see what you can find out. Use all of your senses to try and gather information," Lillian said.

"Okay," said Joe. "You okay with that Izzie?"

"You bet. Let's all split after breakfast. We can follow them out and use our free-time to start our investigation." Izzie was

SOMEONE HAS SOME EXPLAINING TO DO...

finally feeling like part of the group. It felt great until she was corrected by Lillian.

"Conversation. Izzie, we don't want whoever did this to think we are on to them. So, just engage in polite conversation, Nancy Drew style, and see if you can find anything out."

"I can do that," Izzie said, but deep down she was doubtful of her social graces and wasn't sure if she would actually pull this off. If only this were a spelling bee, a math quiz, or a trivia contest, she would have been much more confident. Her new friends needed her though and she was willing to give it her best shot. And besides, she would have Joe with her. "Lillian can I borrow your pen?"

"Sure, why?" Lillian asked as she put the pen forward toward Izzie.

Izzie reached for the pen, ripped part of the letter off for a piece of paper, started writing and said, "Here guys. Try searching these phrases. It may be nothing but it may help." After they made their plan with the boys, the girls snuck out of the cabin and went straight to the mess hall.

The girls were much quieter at breakfast time. Mrs. Mendax had her usual plate of assorted breads and muffins delivered to each table. The corn muffins were the best. They were served at breakfast in the morning and at dinner they were renamed cornbread. They were a camp favourite. Each morning, every table was given a plate of muffins and breads for toasting, jug of juice, jug of water, jug of milk (for drinking or cereal), jellies and preserves, and the main breakfast item. Sometimes it was bacon and eggs. Other times it was sausage and hash browns. One time, it was this breakfast dish that every camper raved about. It had a layer of hash browns on the bottom and topped with a cheesy layer of ham, bacon, and sausage, in a creamy gooey awesome tasting sauce. It smelled like comfort and happiness. Mendax didn't always serve the best food, like oatmeal day, and her sausages were often undercooked and gross, and her bacon was too fatty, but the breakfast casserole was a hit. At least Mendax used fresh farm ingredients from Big P's farm. From the corn to the bacon, Mendax pretty much exclusively used Big P's farm produce and livestock.

Breakfast was nearly finished when Joe nudged Izzie and looked over at the far door. That was the door Izzie always used to get into the mess hall. Vern was leaving. His hand still stained, but you could tell there were attempts to clean it as it was faded compared to earlier that morning. The girls excused themselves from the table and made their way to follow Vern. As they left, Allie saw Fred leaving through the main door.

"Come on Lillian, let's get moving. It's time for free-time."

Lillian was in mid-chew of a corn muffin and just mumbled something that Allie could not possible understand as she got up and left. Heather was left alone at the table. She looked at the empty places around her. No one was there; just her.

Heather looked around and made sure no one was looking. She slowly put her nose down to her left and right armpits. "I showered. I swear." Then she put her nose down to double check. "I did." And then she smiled and watched the kids from cabin 14 clear the table. Their cheer was not good.

As Joe walked down the ramp from the mess hall to follow Vern she noticed Big P and Mendax talking to each other. She pulled on Izzie's shoulder and motioned for Izzie to look at them. Izzie had difficulty hearing them but did catch the words "No...I don't... risky... caught." Izzie tried hard to piece it together. As Izzie and Joe got further from Mendax and Big P, Izzie felt more comfortable taking longer looks to gather more information. Then she heard "Mega Farm". The way the two spoke to each other reminded Izzie of an old married couple. There was obviously some kind of relationship there but it seemed to Izzie that it was love/hate. They loved to hate each other or hated loving each other, either way these two were not in a good relationship. Izzie stopped watching them and refocused on watching Vern. He went into his large green workshop.

"Knock, knock. Can we come in?" Joe said with a smile to Vern.

"Sure kids. You need a hand?" Vern asked.

"I think, I'm good," said Izzie. "Wow, would you look at this place! This is awesome. It's like a science lab in here." Izzie was astonished. What she thought was going to be a glorified broom closet turned out to be the most interesting thing she had seen at camp yet. There were typical garden hoses, extension cords, garden tools, and lawn care products. There were also regular cleaning supplies and appliances. But there was more. There were plants growing in large glass containers. There were pipes of purple, red, and orange going from storage buckets into the base of the plant soil. There were specialized lights and computers on the far wall. On the work bench were several roles of duct tape, tools, measuring tapes, nails and screws. The nails were not like the ones used to hang the letters but there was one box that wasn't open. In the one corner by the computers there was a large electrical panel with a large pipe coming in from the roof directly to the panel. Then under the panel there were a web of wires that went into the ground. A large pad lock with a numbered combination held a fence-like gate shut keeping curious hands from electrocuting themselves. The computer screens had all different things on them. One was a map of the camp with blue lines running across it. Izzie quickly put together that this must run the sprinkler system. The other had something that looked like a graph with several bars that moved up and down ever so slightly. The bars were green. It looked like it might be for power levels. The third computer had a game of chess on the screen. Izzie loved chess. She looked at that screen and quickly deduced that White was going to win in six moves. The last screen had a screen saver on. It flashed old photos, most in black and white, obviously scanned into the computer, and most looked like they were from the camp. One of the old black and white pictures had a group of boys and girls. One of the girls looked very familiar but before Izzie could place her the screen changed to an old picture of a boy with a line of fish he had caught.

"What's this?" Joe asked Vern.

"Oh, that's the sprinkler head I was replacing this morning. Don't touch …"

It was too late. Joe grabbed a hold of the piece before she heard Vern's warning. She immediately dropped it back on to the workbench. She looked down at her right hand, the hand she used to pick it up, and it was ink stained! "Oh my goodness, she did it! She wrote the letters," Izzie thought to herself and in her head she laughed. She only wished that the other girls could have heard her thought. It was pretty clever. Izzie was very clever that way. She could tell that was not often the case with Joe. She was sure that Joe thought things that were clever much faster in her head but seemed to have trouble saying them aloud.

Slowly Joe raised the hand up to Izzie. Izzie smiled and nodded. "Oh look at that mess!" said Izzie.

"Not to worry. I did the same thing this morning. This will take most of the grease off, and the light stain will only last a couple of days. No harm done." He took out an industrial hand cleaner and rag and helped Joe clean up.

"This isn't the worst mess I've seen at this camp. No sir. It must have been 40 years ago. There was one girl, a nice girl, she would have been around your age. She was quiet and loved to pick berries in the forest. She was shy and different. Back then, kids who were different were often the target of bullying and teased a lot. She quickly got the nickname 'Berries' for the amount of her free-time she spent picking blueberries.

Well one day, she came back with two buckets of blueberries. The chef at the time took her in and taught her how to use the berries to make pies for the campers. And they were good pies. After dessert was served that evening, the chef made a point of centering out the little girl and commended her for a great job. The little girl was in her glory. That night, when she went into her bunk and sometime after she had laid her head down on her pillow, she felt something damp against her ear. When she got up, she saw there was a bunch of her blueberry pie slices hidden in her pillow case. It steeped through the pillow case, ruining it, and stained the side of her face and hair. It didn't come out for weeks."

"That's terrible," Izzie said sadly.

"Don't worry Joe, your hand won't be stained for weeks. It will only be a couple days. Promise." He smiled at Joe with a smile of reassurance.

"What happened to the girl?" asked Joe.

"She became bitter and angry. She didn't really trust people again. Our actions can have a serious impact on others. Every good deed can create another good deed, but every bad deed has the potential to create many bad deeds. Evil and fear travels on an easier road than good. To be good, is to take the more difficult road. Now," he paused, "show me the letters you found."

Izzie's heart fell to the floor. "How did you…"

"You are obviously here to see if it was me, and the fact that you're here means it's obviously not you."

"We don't have them," Joe said.

"Ah, smart. Well, were they like this?" Vern took out the letters he had gone around taking off the doors in the morning. He had so many of them. "I assume you have 27, 29, 31, 23 and 38? They were the only doors I did not find letters on. I assumed that it was kids, kids like the kids who hid the pie in the pillowcase, that did it. I suspected that since, 27, 29, 31, 23, and 38 didn't have letters that either they found them or, they wrote them. So, which do you have and perhaps we can figure out who played this trick."

"We have 27, 29, and 38 but not the others!" Izzie felt a sense of relief knowing that the kids in 23, or 31 would be responsible for this. Silly pranksters. Busted pranksters.

"What is going on?" Lillian asked Allie as she heard crying and commotion as they entered the main camp office.

"I just want to go home!" a small camper said.

"You can use the phone after David."

"I want to talk to my parents too. Can't I use your cell phone?"

"You know that we don't get cell service out here. You can call right after... Hello girls. Just give me a minute." The receptionist, Justine, turned back to the commotion, Allie covered her mouth and whispered, "I don't know. Cabin 23 is here and they are not happy."

Lillian took Allie's face in her hands. She mouthed the words 'It sounds like they want to go home' but was careful not to say it out loud for anyone to hear. Allie just read her lips and nodded. Allie looked over and saw Fred's door was open and she grabbed Lillian's arm and while Justine was distracted by the distraught campers, led the way directly into Fred's office.

"Well this isn't going to help Jason. We need the funding or we're going to be in trouble. Now, bring me the paperwork, the best deal you've got. Let me look it over and I'll decide what is best. I appreciate your advice Jason...No...Right. You got it now. I'm sure with the right deal, we'll be here for a while... but get this, I am not selling." Fred was on the phone looking out the window at the camp center. He had a great view of the lake and the center of camp from his office. Lillian heard the entire conversation and looked carefully at Allie and put her finger to her lips. "Shhh" she motioned and Allie nodded.

"Oh dear!" Fred held his chest when he turned around. He had a fitted white sweater over a blue collared shirt. His blond hair and ascot had a familiar heroic look. "Girls, you scared the jeepers out of me." He took several breaths to compose himself. Then he sat at his desk where he hung up his phone. He looked exhausted. "Sit down girls."

The girls sat in the chairs facing Fred.

"Sorry if you making me jump unsettled you."

"Oh we're fine. I always expect the unexpected and loud noises don't bother Allie," Lillian said with maturity and in a business-like manner. She was mature beyond her years. "Why do those campers want to go home?" Lillian asked.

"Well, they are a little home sick."

"Cut the act Fred."

"It's Frank and …"

"Is it because of the letters?" Lillian asked pointedly.

"Letters. You got one too?" He paused. "Right. You are Cabin 29. Vern said 29 was one of the cabins he didn't get to in time. Girls you have been the victim of a prank. But there is no need to worry or be upset."

"Do we look upset?"

"No," Fred sat and looked at Lillian. Her face was cold and ready for answers. No one would want to play cards against her as she definitely had a strong poker face.

"Vern noticed the letters on the doors early in the morning. He got all of them except for a few cabins. We figure the ones he didn't get were most likely the pranksters. Now, the letters are threatening in nature, so as soon as we figure out which cabin it is, sadly the whole cabin's campers will go home. As you could tell, it has already scared the new campers in 23. So, we know that Cabin 23 and 29 are not the pranksters. Fred lifted his pen from his desk and Allie watched as he crossed off 23, 29 off a list. All he had left was 27, ~~29~~, 31, ~~23~~, and 38.

"We have the letters from 27 and 38," Allie pointed at the list. Fred crossed those off. ~~27~~, ~~29~~, **31,** ~~23~~, and ~~38~~. That left cabin 31. "Only cabin left on the list is 31," said Allie.

"Girls, keep this quiet. Until I talk to them, I would prefer if you kept this to yourselves. You do that and I won't ask how you got the letter from 38, a boy's cabin. The girl's shrunk in their seats a little and agreed that that was a very fair deal. Fred got up and walked to the door of his office. He put on his camper's vest and hat.

"I trust since you girls were able to find your way into my office that you'll be able to find your way out?" He winked, nodded, and left.

The girls motioned like they were getting up to leave and as soon as Fred left, Allie said "He's gone."

"Allie, look at his desk. I want to know if there is anything about that phone call there. I'll stand by the door."

"But it's the kids from 31. Why?" Allie got up as she questioned and looked at all the documents on his desk. "I have no idea what these mean." She took out her cell phone and took pictures of them.

"I hear someone coming," Lillian whispered and waved at Allie. She put her ear to the edge of the door. "It sounds like Justine's heading toward the office." Lillian waved her hand at Allie again. Allie took her last picture and headed for the office door to leave with Lillian. They bumped into Justine at the door.

"Oh girls, sorry about that but you can't just come into Frank's office, you'll have to wait here in these chairs," Justine said pointing to the reception area.

"Oh that's fine, we'll just come back later," Lillian said. Allie and her left in a hurry.

Justine looked into Fred's office, sighed and closed his door. "That man is never around. I have to do everything."

CHAPTER VII

Banker stakes his claim...

"'POSSIBLE MOTIVES FOR SCARING PEOPLE are: money, power, treasure, and bullying.' It says here 'The main reason for group scares are usually pranks and thrills. If the scare is expected it is likely for a thrill, like a scary campfire story. If it is unexpected by the audience, then it is most likely for a prank. People who scare others often want power over their victims. Other common reasons are to gain financially with money, land or some other treasure that the person or persons doing the scaring want.'" Eliot read.

"Let's try this other one that Izzie wrote down, 'Big schemes to scare people,'" Lucas said.

"Hmmm this one says, 'Elaborate schemes are rare and even more rarely successful when trying to scare someone. We learned in the world of Scooby Doo that evil plans with complicated plots rarely succeed, and in real life, evil plans are usually simple. When trying to plan, mastermind criminals often try to find the beauty in simplicity. The simpler the master plan, the more genius it is.' Ugh. More Scooby Doo stuff. I don't know Lucas, this seems pretty complicated. It's probably just a prank and not a master plan to scare us. What do you think?"

Lucas, looking over Eliot's shoulder at his tablet, sighed. "I don't know either. I'd say your right, that it's probably just some kids playing a prank."

"Do you think the girls are pretending to be on our side just to scare us even more?"

"No. You saw Joe. She's freaked out," Lucas got up and looked out his window. "Come on. We're going to be late for our session. Free-time is over. Do you have a session with 29 today?"

"Ya, archery," said Eliot, as he continued looking at his tablet.

"Okay, let the girls know that we will come to their cabin tonight and we can all share information."

"Well, we have more information to share… look!"

Lucas went over and stared at the tablet. His eyes widened. "Whoa."

Fred opened the door to cabin 31.

"Alright boys…"

Before he could finish his sentence, he was attacked by a bear. His face was impacted by a furry, fluffy, teddy bear with big button eyes. Another hit him in the stomach. Then came the water bottles. They were open and Fred got soaked. One hit him square in the middle of his shorts and it looked like he had an accident. The pillows followed. The one that was full of feathers was particularly heavy and jarred Fred's head around. A barrage of water balloons followed. Now Fred looked like a soaked rag doll. The assault continued. Little boys, around the age of nine charged Fred as he fell to his knees covering his face with his arms. Several cabin dwellers shook cans of soda and cracked them open in Fred's direction and others took gummie worms and dumped them on his drenched body. Once they unloaded all their ammunition, the boys quickly retreated behind their fort. The bunks were repositioned and mattresses were turned to create a barricade between the boys and the door.

"Enough, it's me Frank!"

There was a moment of silence and stillness. A gummie worm slid down Fred's cheek and hit the wet floor with a splat.

"Fred?" a little voice called out.

"Yes. Fine. Fred," he said as he stood up and composed himself.

"We thought you were the monster who wrote this letter," said another little boy. The littlest in the cabin.

"You have a letter?" Fred asked. "So you *didn't* write them," he said under his breath.

"Ya. Once we got it, we made a fort to protect ourselves. It was Dylan's idea!" said one boy. The boys looked horrified like they were probably in big trouble.

"Was not!" said Dylan who was in trouble more than once last year and was all too familiar with Fred's office and phone calls home.

"Boys. It's fine. Clean this mess up. This letter is just a harmless prank. Clean up and get to session one. I've got to get cleaned up myself. And boys, not a word about the letter to any other campers, or this," he said pointing to how terrible he looked, "will be dealt with in my office. Understand?"

"Yes Fred," they all said.

"It's Fran…. Oh never mind. Get this place cleaned up." As he shut the door behind him, he laughed a little then looked at the letter. His smile went away and he made his way back to his cabin.

The next day went pretty normal. After breakfast was session one and then snack in the outdoor pavilion. Afterward was session two and then lunch in the mess hall. After lunch was session three and four, then cabin clean up, inspection from counsellors, and then it was off to dinner in the mess hall. Finally, the campers went to camp circle around the fire and off to their cabins for bed time routines. Everything was robotic and normal but lacked a certain camp chemistry. All the staff seemed on edge and just went through the motions with no real effort or the typical camp passion that they usually had.

During session two, the girls of 29 had archery with Eliot and a bunch of other campers. The archery setup consisted of six circular targets lined up about a table width apart. There were rows of yellow nylon ropes that made lanes from the shooting line to the target. Heather modeled how to shoot from the shooting line in lane one. She pulled back the arrow and held it for a long time. Izzie watched as Heather controlled her breathing, kept her arms still and let go of the quiver. It made a cool noise as it flew through the air and impaled into the target backed by giant hay stacks. Izzie intensely watched the lesson until she was interrupted by Eliot.

"Hey, Lucas wants you to know that we are coming to your cabin tonight."

"Where is Lucas?" Izzie asked.

"Soccer. Why?" Eliot asked.

"Just curious," Izzie said hoping that her curiosity of Lucas wouldn't tip Eliot off about the new feelings Izzie was feeling every time Lucas was near. She looked up at Eliot from the corner of her eyes and he was fixated on Heather. Eliot had completed his mission at the session just like Lucas had asked.

Kids were allowed to sign up for different sessions at the beginning of camp. The girls from 29, all but Izzie, signed up for the same things, however after day two, Allie asked Heather, who in turn asked Justine, to make the switch so that Izzie could be in all their sessions too. Justine made the switch rather easily. Eliot and Lucas had different interests. Lucas liked more team activities, like soccer, and Eliot liked things he could do more solo, like archery. However, it should be noted that Heather was the leader for 75% of Eliot's sessions. Interesting.

After bedtime routines and 'lights out' was called for across the camp, Eliot and Lucas got ready to sneak out and head to 29. The campers were explicitly told not to leave their cabins for any reason until a counsellor came and got them in the morning. Eliot and Lucas looked at each other before leaving the cabin. The boys knew their way through the woods and would easily be able to stay off the path in order to avoid being caught. They had planned everything and knew that they would have to be extra alert that night but what happened next they did not anticipate.

When they opened their door there was a sound like pants ripping. They looked up and saw duct tape on their door, torn in half. How would they ever be able to put it back from the inside of the cabin? They looked at the cabin across the path from them. It too had duct tape on the corner of their door. If any campers opened their door the tape would rip and the counsellors would know.

"What do we do?" Eliot whispered.

"I don't know but there's no going back now. The damage is done."

"I don't want to get kicked out of camp," Eliot said.

"Me either. But there is nothing we can do about this right now. We'll worry about it when we get back from the girl's cabin."

"We're going to be so busted," said Eliot and the boys ducked into the woods and headed for Cabin 29.

Cabin 29 had tape on their door too but at least the boys could take it off and put it back when they left to save the girls from getting into trouble. With a soft knock and tape in their hand, the boys were let into Cabin 29.

"What did you find out?" Lucas asked Lillian.

"It's not Vern or Fred. The ink on Vern's hand was grease from a sprinkler head and he already knew about the letters. Apparently, all the cabins had letters. Vern got all the letters except from a few, and the ones we got. Fred narrowed it down to 31 and said he was going to confront them but it obviously wasn't them because they were at lunch and dinner today."

"Not to mention that they duct taped us all in our cabins," Lucas said. "If they knew who it was, they wouldn't be doing this."

"The kids from 23 went home. Once one left, they all left," Eliot said.

"No, I heard that Stevie just moved to cabin 31," said Lucas.

"Ya, I heard that too. One of the guys, Dylan, from 31, told me at soccer today," said Joe.

"So, if the guys from 23 or 31 didn't do it, Vern didn't do it, Fred didn't do it, who did it?" Allie asked.

"Izzie and I saw Medax and Big P talking today," said Joe.

"Ya, they were kind of arguing by the side entrance." Izzie said.

"They always fight," laughed Lilian.

"But this was different. I heard the words 'No…I don't… risky… caught…and mega farm.'"

Everyone was quiet. Puzzled. "This is too confusing and how are we going to get back into our cabin and put tape on the outside of the door?" Eliot asked.

"I've got that figured out," Izzie, like playing chess, was several steps ahead of the others. "Before you go back though, and I solve your tape puzzle, did you guys find out anything online?"

"Yes!" Eliot said. "We looked up all this stuff for motives for scaring people like Izzie suggested and all this psychobabble came up. One of the reasons was money. So, I went to a real estate site where you can buy homes, to see how much this camp would be worth. We are talking over a million dollars."

"So, what does the camp value have to do with scaring us?" Allie asked. "And here, I took these pictures on my cell see if you can make sense of them."

"You have a cell phone?" asked Eliot.

"I have needs too Eliot," said Allie with a smile. She air-dropped them to his tablet as there was no cell signal to text or email them.

"Because," Izzie brought the conversation back to Allie's original question, "if the campers leave, it ruins Fred's camp. If Fred's camp is ruined he would probably have to sell it. Someone could get this land cheap."

"But Fred loves this camp," sighed Joe.

"We all do," said Lillian.

"Doesn't that seem a bit farfetched?" asked Allie.

"No. It's simple. And all it costs the person doing this is some envelopes and paper."

"Simple! That's what Google said. Online it said that evil plans are never like in the movies. They are actually always quite simple. That's the genius of them," Eliot said excitedly.

"Right," said Lucas in a calming voice, as to settle Eliot down. "So, how do we get back in our room exactly? There's no way we can fix the tape Izzie or put it back on the door from the inside of the cabin."

Izzie looked up and smirked. "Here's what you're going to do..."

The next morning, as planned, Vern went into Fred's office about an hour before sunrise so that they could look to see if there were letters on any of the cabin doors and to see if any duct tape was ripped.

"Morning Fred," Vern said with a smirk.

"Morning Charlie," Fred said to Vern. "I figure if you're not going to me Frank, then I'm not calling you Vern."

"Shall we check our traps?" smiled Vern.

"Let's go." Fred put on his camper's hat and vest and left the office with Vern. They went out the side door of the camp office, down the ramp, to the main path. The moon was still shining brightly and the birds were not awake yet. No one was. The camp was still. On the way to the path that led to the cabins, there was an inuksuk welcoming the campers. It stood about three feet tall with six rocks making its height. Vern and Fred stopped and stared at it. Fred shook his head. Vern laughed.

"Clever," said Fred, "I'm going back to bed." And he turned and left.

"G'nite sir," Vern chuckled. He walked over to the inuksuk. From the surface of the top rock he lifted a large ball of tape. The tape was removed from every door. There were no letters nailed to any of the doors that night.

Later that morning there was a rumble in the air as the campers awoke. The campers were told explicitly to stay in their cabins until the counsellors came and got them. Many of the campers broke this rule once they woke up. The commotion outside prompted Lillian to wake up Allie.

"What do you think is going on?" Lillian asked Allie.

Allie and Joe got out of their beds and looked out the window. There were kids, still in their pyjamas running to the counsellor's cabin.

"Look!" Izzie from her bed pointed at the floor by the cabin door. There was a letter that was slid under the door. Allie reached down and picked it up. She sat on Izzie's bunk and read.

"Your days are numbered. Leave! Heed my warning!"

Izzie felt sick.

"Maybe we should go? This is getting kind of serious," said Allie.

Lillian took charge. "No. I'm not letting someone affect how I feel. I will not let someone try to put fear in my life. I'm sure that whoever is doing this wants us to be scared and wants us to leave. And that's exactly why we have to stay. Are you girls with me?"

"We are the..." Izzie started. The rest of the girls joined in.

"...cabin, that makes, cabin friends so great. We are the cabin that makes, cabin friends so great!"

The girls waited, as instructed from the night before, for Heather to arrive at the cabin and get the girls for breakfast. When she arrived Izzie noticed that Heather was not so chipper. She looked concerned and must have asked the girls a thousand times if they were alright and if they were scared. Heather kept reassuring the girls that everything would be alright but Izzie wasn't scared at all and only wanted to get to the bottom of what was going on and why.

"Girls, everything is okay. I'm sure that it's just some loser who likes to scare people," Heather said and she looked over at a couple of CITs (counsellors in training), Jimmie and Brian who were across from the girl's cabin on the main pathway. They were talking and playfully punching each other.

"Are you trying to convince us, or yourself?" Lillian asked.

"Honestly, a little of both," Heather said still watching the boys through the cabin window. Izzie looked over at the CITs and back at Heather. She obviously had her suspicions of these boys by why? Izzie made a mental note of Heather's behaviour and ruled her out as a suspect.

Allie didn't appear to hear a word Heather said or deliberately changed the subject, "I like the cute accessories you're wearing. They're all matchie matchie."

"I smell breakfast," Joe said, "It's the casserole!" She smiled.

Izzie took the social cue that no one wanted to talk about this anymore and everyone made their way to the mess hall together. Heather stared down the boys who went very quiet when the girls went by. Izzie watched carefully and felt like the boys were up to something but nothing came of it.

On the way into the mess hall this time, Izzie heard Mendax talking to Fred.

"He thought that we would stop buying our produce from him and got all up in my face. Kept talking about us breaking a contract to buy cheaper stuff from a mega farm."

"I'll talk to him. We've dealt with him for years. We're not buying anything from another farm," Fred said.

"He's paranoid. I kept tellin' him that but he's not believin' me."

"Well, if these letters keep coming, there won't be any campers left here to buy food for. Just leave it with me," said Fred.

"He says he's got a plan to help. I say he's nuttier than squirrel turd."

"A plan?" said Fred.

"A plan," said Mendax.

Izzie made her way in the side door completely unnoticed by Mendax and Fred. When Heather left the table to make her toast, Izzie shared the latest information with the girls. Then she got her first taste of Mendax's famous casserole.

Despite Mrs. Mendax preparing the camp favourite, Izzie noticed a lot of campers were missing.

"Where is everyone?" Izzie asked.

"Waiting in line at the office for Justine's phone to call home. The youngest campers," Allie said nodding in the direction of tables of little ones, "are not old enough to know what's going on, so unless they have a scared older brother or sister, they're mostly fine. The oldest ones," she nodded at the tables with teens, "don't seem to care and just laugh it off as a joke."

Heather returned to the table and obviously heard Allie's awkwardly loud voice and continued Allie's thought, "It is the ones who are old enough to understand the letters, but young enough to buy into the threat that are the most scared."

"Like us," said Lillian.

"And sadly for Fred and his camp, that's the bulk of his campers." Heather said. Izzie looked around and noticed a lot of empty chairs in the mess hall.

After dealing with the families of several of the campers who wanted to leave, Fred went over to Jason who was waiting in his office for him. Fred motioned for Jason to join him outside where things were less chaotic. Fred and Jason walked quickly down the path toward the canoes. Jason was the local banker that held Fred's accounts. He didn't look like a typical banker. You picture most bankers as wearing dark suits and slick hair. No, Jason looked more like a movie star. He wore a bright purple golf shirt, so neat and pressed that it looked brand new. He had silver mirrored sunglasses on, with crisp beige pants and fancy shoes. He didn't look like he belonged in a camp, but on a set of the latest blockbuster movie. He was young, for a bank executive, and very physically fit. His watch looked like it cost a million dollars. He held a slick portfolio case with some professional papers in it. On the side of the case were several pens and a stylus for his tablet, which was so slim and high-tech that it looked like a piece of space paper. Fred was looking over paperwork. He was reading while walking. He was in his traditional camp garb but he was clean shaven and looked a little more awake than yesterday.

Jason couldn't have come at a worse time. When he showed up earlier, the office was full of campers wanting to go home and Justine was at her wit's end. If the camp wasn't making money, Fred would have difficulty securing the loan he would need to keep the camp. Once word went viral on the internet about the letters, his camp's reputation would take a hit and he might lose even more campers.

Izzie and Allie were heading to their cabin when they saw this newcomer who was with Fred. They slowed their pace and watched them from afar. Allie could not hear them but watched their mouths.

"Who is that?" Izzie asked.

"I'm trying to find out," Allie replied.

"Using telepathy?"

"I'm reading their lips. I can do that. If I can see their mouths I'll know what they are saying. It's like having super hearing without hearing at all. I'll tell you what they are saying."

Izzie watched as Allie worked her magic.

"This looks good" said Fred. "Why the revenue audit though?"

"If we are going to lend you the money you need, we need to make sure that our interests are covered," Jason said.

"I've never let you down before Jason."

"No, Frank, but times are tight, and we need to make sure that you have enough money coming in to cover your expenses and this new loan."

"I'll have Justine get everything ready."

Jason turned and his back was now facing Izzie and Allie. Something was said and Izzie watched them shake hands and smile. Then Izzie saw that as Jason walked away from Fred, Fred's face turned worrisome. When Izzie and Allie got back to the cabin, Allie reported what she saw to the rest of the girls. Joe, in turn, told the boys at a session later that day.

On the way to dinner, the girls saw Big P talking with Heather. She looked thrilled. Heather hugged Big P and ran toward the office. Mr. Perdas smiled and went back to unloading his produce for Mrs. Mendax's kitchen. Heather was a little late getting to dinner but seemed to be back to her regular self.

"Guess what girls?" she said enthusiastically.

"What?" Lillian said with a smile.

"Mr. Perdas has a plan!"

"You know about that?" asked Joe.

"Yes. He just told me his master plan. Wait. How do you know the plan?"

Izzie thought quickly once again. "We just know that he is up to something. He is always planning something with Mendax...right?"

Looking a little confused, Heather went on, "Well this has nothing to do with Mendax. We're going to his farm tomorrow after breakfast. All the campers will take a hay ride to his farm and spend the day there. For lunch he is making a big bonfire and we can roast hot dogs and marshmallows. We can pet the animals, ride the horses, milk the cows…"

"Hold on. I'm not milking a cow," said Allie. "I clearly don't have a 'milk the cow' outfit here."

Everyone laughed and it was exactly what Heather knew would take all the camper's minds off the letters. And she was right. Everyone was excited about the field trip especially Izzie who had never been to a farm before. She was excited to see cows, chickens, pigs, the barn, water well, and all the crops growing.

CHAPTER VIII

Where be that girl...

"DOES THIS OUTFIT SAY 'FARM girl cute' or 'Farm girl worker'?" asked Allie as she posed for Joe and Izzie. She wore overall shorts with a plaid t-shirt on underneath with red ribbons in her pig tails.

"It says 'I don't understand farming,'" replied Joe.

"I like it," said Izzie. "Do you have any more ribbons?" Izzie already knew the answer to the question. She had eyed Allie's ribbon collection on day one but was waiting for the perfect opportunity to politely ask. With all the cabin had shared now, Izzie felt like a welcomed part of the group. No one spoke much about Alex anymore. Izzie was a perfect fit despite her differences.

"Here, wear these," Allie handed Izzie two blue ribbons. The material was dark and shiny on one side and light blue on the underneath side. Izzie made a tiny ponytail in the front right side of her hair. The ribbons, one at the base of the pony tail and one in the middle were tied in symmetrical bow ties. They were small and adorable and more importantly they made Izzie feel welcomed and cute.

With the girls all ready to go, Allie led the way holding on to Lillian's arm. Lillian took a deep breath.

"Hay!" she said.

"What?" asked Allie.

"No, not hey, hay. H-A-Y. I smell hay and lots of it," Lillian smiled.

"Well I hope you like it because you'll be sitting on it. Oh my outfit is going to be so mad at me for this." And with that, Allie plunked herself down on the haystack.

The smell the hay on the big wagon behind the camp tractor seemed to overpower the smell of the diesel fumes created by the tractor's engine. Joe walked behind Izzie and helped her onto the wagon. The wagon had about 40 of the campers sitting along the perimeter and about 20 in the middle. The haystacks made for great seating and also provided a rectangular pathway for the kids to walk and find places to sit. The campers in the middle sat back-to-back facing the perimeters of the wagon while the kids on the outside haystacks looked inward and had to strain themselves to twist and see the scenery on the way to Mr. Perdas' farm while adhering to the 'feet on the floor' rule.

The camp van passed the slow tractor several times delivering supplies and counsellors to the farm. Each time it passed the wagon, the counsellors would scream and wave. There were no seats in the back of the van and it traveled with the rear doors open to allow for the long pieces of wood that would be used for benches to sit of at the Farm's bonfire. There were always a lot of counsellors and CITs in the back of the van that tossed about the back of the van. If it wasn't a dirt road, the camp would have never allowed passengers in the cargo van.

Izzie was at the back by the wagon's gate. Joe sat next to her. The campers laughed and told stories on the bumpy trip. The wagon seemed to jolt everyone in the air like a carnival ride when there was a large bump in the road, which was often. Every time it happened, the campers cheered. Heather would lock eyes on the other counsellors on the hay ride and make funny faces when she was propelled off her haystack by the bumps.

"What are you doing?" Izzie shouted over the loud tractor and other campers.

"I'm counting the kids to make sure none of them fell off the wagon," Heather laughed, "You wouldn't want us to lose you, would you?"

"No!" laughed Izzie.

Heather would joke on the first day of camp when greeting the parents in the parking lot during orientation that she would only lose one or two campers a trip and that was a 90-96% success rate; an A+, if it were a school grade. This always made parents laugh and seemed to make them more comfortable as they were leaving their children in the care of these young camp counsellors.

The kids cheered again when they hit yet another bump on the dirt road that sent them soaring up in the air and then crashing down. Izzie really had a great time on the ride. She looked up as the tractor drove under the big sign that said 'Holiday Farms est 1929'. It framed the laneway leading into the farm area. The driveway leading into the farm was in nicer condition than the town road. The farm was immaculate. Izzie was in awe.

Lillian said, "The smells of all the flowers and produce are amazing."

Allie said, "Look at the beautiful colors of the flowers and the huge barn!"

Izzie said, "Over there! I see the animals!"

Joe said, "I see lunch!"

Izzie looked up in horror at Joe. "How could you say that about the beautiful farm animals?"

Joe looked down at Izzie and Izzie made sure that Joe knew that she was not impressed by giving her a scrunched up face of disapproval.

"No, not the animals. Look a buffet table is being set. Mmmmm." Joe rubbed her tummy with pleasure and pointed where the lunch table was being set up. The table was actually many tables linked together and was being set by the counsellors who volunteered to help Big P. "I love barbecued hotdogs," Joe continued.

Izzie looked less distressed and decided a sarcastic smirk might do better.

"Well, at least with hotdogs you are never really sure which farm animal you're eating," Joe said trying to justify her love of food.

Izzie just laughed and took in the beautiful scenery.

The tractor came to a stop and, after everyone was unloaded, it went back to the camp to get the remaining campers. The kids were divided into groups and the counsellors were assigned to watch over a group. Big P gave each counsellor a map with a schedule. They would go to each section of the farm and participate in different activities. Big P addressed all the campers in a large field before dismissing them for their first activity. He thanked them for being there and welcomed them with a large bold voice. He explained where the food the campers ate came from and that farming was a noble profession.

"Farms feed cities!" he shouted. "Make sure you take care of your farmers and don't forget about us when you head back home in a couple of weeks."

"Do you kill the pigs here?" a voice yelled out from the crowd. "Cuz I like bacon but I ain't killin no pig."

Some in the crowd laughed. Big P just smiled and said, "No. We raise our livestock, then we ship them out for 'processing'. I haven't had to kill anything on this farm in quite some time and when a sacrifice is made, it should be done quickly and with a heavy heart. The place that does that ships the product back here for me to sell, distribute, and eat. I run just a small local farm. The kind of thing you are talking about would require a farm five times this size." Then he continued with his prepared opening remarks.

A counsellor went over to the boy who shouted the question and whispered something to him that seemed to make the young camper feel rather sheepish. He didn't ask another question for the rest of the day without raising his hand first.

For the first time in their short stay at the camp, the girls were separated into different groups and for the first time in quite a few hours, Izzie was not thinking about the letters. Izzie watched as Joe left with a group that was going to start in the section of the farm where the chickens are fed. Allie was sent to milk the cows. Izzie laughed and thought, "At least she has the right outfit for it." however, Allie looked horrified. Finally, Izzie watched as Lillian's group went to the pig pens. Izzie was sure that the smell of the boy's cabin would adequately prepare Lillian for the smell of the pig pen.

Izzie's group was led to the pond where the ducks and sheep were. Izzie felt isolated. She was not with one camper she had met before and the counsellor was one of the two boys that Heather was suspicious of just a day ago, Brian. The other girls knew their counsellors and the campers in their groups were all familiar to them. The camp wasn't that big after all. Izzie found that Brian wasn't very supportive either.

Izzie looked across the pond and saw where the rapids met the stillness of the pond. She looked further upstream and saw small valley where Joe had almost fallen into the rapids. Her eyes gazed at the beauty of what seemed so terrifying just days ago when Joe hung on for dear life. Izzie was looking at the trail circled the pond and traveled into the distance by the rapids when she was rudely interrupted by a duck that quacked at her and made her jolt. Then it happened. Izzie had to pee.

"I have to use the facilities," Izzie said to Brian, who was distracted by scaring sheep and chasing ducks.

Without even looking at Izzie he replied, "So go."

"Where?"

"The farmhouse I guess," he said still only focused on chasing the animals and making weird noises. Frustrated, Izzie turned toward the farmhouse. It was about 30 yards past an old well.

It was the last time Izzie was seen on that trip.

At lunch, things were hectic. Groups ate at different times, as the farm was not equipped for feeding such a large group of people all at once. Lunch was all part of the rotation on the schedule Big P made. The afternoon lunch schedule was rudely interrupted. Clouds in the sky, in mere minutes, turned dark. The air grew cold. The leaves on the trees flipped showing their light green underbellies when the wind blew. Then there was the crack of thunder and a flash of lightning.

Kids ran to the tractor. They were drenched. Counsellors put campers on the wagon as quickly as they could. It was chaos. The campers who didn't get on the first tractor shuttle split up and ran to the barn and the duck shelter. They were cold and wet. Some were frightened and others were fascinated by the intensity of the storm. Big P was nowhere to be found. Most figured he took shelter in his farmhouse. He lived alone there.

In the darkness of the storm, Allie peered through the crack in the large door of the farm where she had taken shelter and looked at the house on the hill. There was a single light on in the bottom corner window. The flowers that hung on the green porch that wrapped around the farmhouse swayed in the wind, barely hanging on to their hooks. Lillian, Joe, and Izzie were not in the barn. Neither was Heather. Allie was surrounded by other campers and counselors but in many ways was alone and cold. The storm got worse.

The second time the camp tractor returned, the kids from the duck shelter were raced out and put on the wagon to head back to camp. Then it was Allie's turn with the rest of the campers that were in the barn. As the third and last shipment of campers returned to Camp Candle Lake, they were instructed to go directly to their cabins. The rains seem to travel sideways and it made speaking and moving very difficult. The ones who could run, did. Allie ran. It was pouring rain.

Counsellors went to the cabins in their charge to do a head count. When Heather arrived at Cabin 29 her eyes widened and she held her tummy. There were only three campers. Allie, Lillian, and Joe were changed and dry with the exception of their hair. Lillian had a towel and was trying to tend to her wet head. Joe looked up at Heather.

"Where's Izzie?" asked Joe.

"She's not here?" Heather shouted.

"No," Lillian said with concern in her voice.

"We figured that she was in the mess hall or office with you," Allie said.

"Don't play around girls! Izzie!" Heather looked around the cabin frantically but in vain. "Something's wrong," she said under her breath.

"What?" asked Joe.

"Nothing. Girls, I'm sure that she is just in one of the other cabins. Don't worry. I'll get her." Heather closed the door behind her and ran to the cabins she hadn't yet checked to see if Izzie was in one of them. She wasn't. Heather double checked the remaining cabins and the common areas like the mess hall.

Lillian put her towel down. She turned toward the other girls. "Was Izzie with either of you at all today?"

"After Big P gave his welcome speech we all went into different groups," Allie said.

"Ya, I'm pretty sure she was supposed to be in my lunch group," said Joe.

"Were you in mine? I was in second lunch," said Lillian.

"Ya, I was supposed to be in second lunch, but lunch never happened. Of all the times to have a storm." Thunder clapped as Joe complained.

"What if Izzie never made it back?" Allie asked.

"Was she on your tractor ride back?"

"Definitely not and mine was the last one," Allie said.

"Not on mine and I was on the first one back," Joe said.

"And she wasn't on mine and I was on the second ride," Lillian said. "We had to wait in the duck and sheep shelter. I didn't notice her there."

"A bunch of us were in the barn and she wasn't there either," Allie said.

"Heather did look really freaked out," said Joe.

"Well, if you guys never saw her and I definitely didn't notice her then she is definitely back at that farm."

"Heather will find her right?" Joe asked with concern in her voice.

"Yes, and when she does, we will be there too," Lillian said and another flash of lightning filled their cabin and crack of thunder shook the floors.

"How could you not find out where she was?" Heather grilled Brian, the counsellor who was supposed to take care of Izzie, but he didn't seem to care.

"I figured she just wanted to be in a group with her friends. I don't know. Why? What's wrong? She's probably just in the mess hall or something," he said dismissively.

"Oh my gosh..." Heather ran to the office to get the keys to the camp cargo van. Her feet were heavy from the mud created by the intense storm. Fighting her way through the rain with her eyes near tears, Heather burst into the camp office.

"Heather?" queried Justine.

Heather was shaking as she grabbed the keys to the van from the master key rack and ran back into the storm.

"Fred?" Justine watched Heather run out as she called to her boss in his office. "I think there's a problem."

The rain pounded the roof of the van. The wipers could barely keep up with the rain as it crashed on the windshield. Heather was breathing heavily and whispering to herself. "Please be okay... please be okay...please be okay..." The van echoed as its hollow rear cabin made the sound of the water on the roof seem more intense than it probably was. There was a box of straps, blankets, and bungie cords in the very back that slid across the van floor with every turn.

Heather reached in to her coat pocket to grab her cell phone. Her wet hand fumbled the phone as the other hand held tight to the steering wheel. As she lifted the phone to see if she had service on the forest road the van jolted from a pot hole and the phone slipped from her fingers and slid along the rusty steel floor to the back of the van into the pile of blankets. The large lump of blankets in the back would hop in the air when the van hit bumps in the road like the kids on the hay ride. Then it got smooth. The farm road was welcomed relief for the van's precious cargo.

As Heather leapt out of the van and ran through the mud toward the old farm house everything went quiet. Inside the van there was the clicking of engine wires that were cooling from the intense ride to the farm. A Camp Candle Lake air freshener, hanging on the mirror, swayed from side to side still moving from the energy created from the ride. The hollow rear of the van laid empty with the smell of gasoline and chemicals that Vern used to keep the camp looking great and running smooth. The blankets piled on the cold steel floor of the van held the smell of the fumes and would be retired soon for they long outlived their purpose. They moved. The blankets tossed and squirmed like they were about to burst. The frayed ends whipped back and they became a three-headed monster... the cutest three-headed blanket monster ever.

"We've got to be here," Joe whispered.

"Oh my goodness! These blankets smell so bad I think I would rather be in the boy's cabin again," Lillian whispered in disgust.

"There is no outfit for what I just endured," Allie said. She appeared to be completely in shock from the smell and from the way her and her friends were tossed around in the back of the van.

"Guys, focus!" Joe commanded. "We have to make sure that Izzie is okay."

"Well, Heather is just going to kill us when she sees us anyway, so even if Izzie is okay, we're dead," Lillian said.

Joe looked horrified.

"I mean, Izzie is okay and we will be too. Don't worry Joe. Now, find a way out the back of the van for me." Lillian reassured with a comforting tone. It helped the others when

Lillian took charge. Allie reached for Heather's cell phone that slid to the back of the van. There was no service. She checked her own phone and again, no service. The rain was not nearly as intense as when they arrived. As the girls left through the small opening of the rear van doors, they peered around the corner of the van.

"What do you see?" Joe asked Allie.

"Heather is up at the farm house knocking on the doors and windows." Allie pulled her hoodie down over her forehead, turned and fixed Lillian's for her. Joe put her hood up to stop the rain from soaking her hair any further. Her feet sounded squishy in the mud when she moved them. It was wet, dark and muddy.

"If Heather is up at the house then we should go to the barn and look there." Lillian said.

"But the last time I saw her she was near the sheep stable by the pond and water well," Joe interrupted.

"But we didn't see her in those places before we left," Allie said.

"No, but if she was left behind, those would be the best places for shelter."

"Do you guys want to split up?" We'll never make it to both places and back to the van before Heather gets back," Lillian asked with an air of concern in her voice.

"I know what that means. It means that Allie will go with you and yours truly, Joe, will go with the words of 'good luck' or 'you can do this' from you guys. Well forget it." Joe looked impressed with herself at how well she articulated her feelings.

Allie looked at Lillian for a reaction. "Joe," said Lillian, "I know it would mean that you would have to look alone…

in the darkening sky… in the rain… in the mud… with the creepy animals, but it's our new friend Izzie."

"Sure," said Joe hoping that Allie or Lillian would protest.

"Okay, Allie and I will check out the barn and you head to the stable by the pond." Lillian said.

Joe rolled her eyes but the girls did not see her.

As Joe turned away to head to the stable, Lillian grabbed her shoulder awkwardly. Was she going to change her mind about splitting up? Did she figure out where Izzie was?

"Hey. Good luck," Lillian said.

"You can do this," Allie said. They were off in an instant toward the barn.

Joe shook her head, smirked, and darted for the stable.

At Big P's farmhouse, Heather knocked on the door repeatedly. She would scamper over to the windows and try to look in but the lighting outside didn't allow for her to see anything other than shapes and outlines of furniture, none of which looked like Izzie. She turned around with her hands on her hips, still breathing heavily from the running and panic of losing Izzie. From the porch, through the rain, she could see Big P's tractor, car, and delivery truck. It didn't seem like he had left. She walked around the side of the house.

The green porch suddenly seemed old and the tired wood creaked with every step she took. Large drops of water fell on the porch railing from the roof of the house. She came across the screen door to the kitchen. It was framed in the same old wood used for the floorboards of the porch. The screen was dark and it was difficult to see through. The door behind it was not closed. Then, like how a lighthouse in a storm signals a lost ship, Heather's eyes fell upon a white phone hanging on the wall.

The phone was old like one you'd find at a grandmother's house, but it was hardwired and would work, unlike any cell phone in the area. Heather pulled on the screen door, all the while calling for Mr. Perdas to help her. The door was stuck a little when she pulled on it but it came loose and opened and she headed right for the phone. She took the phone in her hand.

Heather's eyes danced around the room. There was a calendar on the wall of the kitchen next to the fridge. There was a picture of a family and under the picture it had the phrase 'Mom knows best!' and she started to dial a number. "Someone be home. I need the camp number. Please be home! I've got to call Fred and let him know what's going on." Her eyes continued to dance around the kitchen. Her eyes passed the kitchen table and its contents. Then they fixated on the fridge and then back to the kitchen table. Then she stared and her eyes widened. With an exhausted exhale, she was able to only whisper "Oh my gosh…" and she dropped the phone.

Allie searched high and low in the barn. Lillian stood by the door as if keeping notice for anyone approaching.

"Anything yet?" asked Lillian.

"What?" Allie replied, not being able to make out what Lillian said.

Lillian exaggerated her voice and mouth movements. "Have you found anything yet? Any sign of Izzie?"

"No. I looked in the loft and the creepy storage area under the barn. I have dirt all over me, I'm cold, wet, and I just want to go back to the camp. Actually, I just want to go home."

Lillian opened her arms to hug Allie and Allie was all too ready to be hugged.

"I hope Izzie is okay," Allie said.

"I'm sure she is fine. She is probably in the farmhouse with Heather and Mr. Perdas." Lillian said comfortingly.

Allie pried open the barn door enough to have a good angle to see the farmhouse. "Heather is not at the farmhouse!"

"Is she going back to the van? Does she have Izzie with her? She didn't leave without us did she?"

"What? Slow down Lillian. No, she didn't leave. I can't see her at all. She was on the porch. She isn't there anymore."

"Maybe she's inside. Can you see somewhere we can hide near the house?"

Allie looked, and saw the perfect spot to hide under a ramp that went up to the porch. She grabbed Lillian's arm and said, "Come on!"

Joe arrived at the stable and went inside. There was plenty of life inside, but none of it was humanoid. She examined the mud floor. She saw lots of animal tracks and some footprints but there were no marks in the mud that would show that Izzie had been there recently. Surprisingly she moved calmly and appeared to be comfortable with the situation. It may have been her innocence or perhaps her positive outlook, but whatever it was, Joe appeared to be at peace… until she turned around.

In the farmhouse kitchen, Heather's eyes could not move from what she saw on the table. It was plans to expand the farm with the land from Camp Candle Lake. More disturbing were the letters and envelopes that were not yet delivered to the campers. The house was silent. Heather trembled. She held her breath. Slowly she turned her head toward the screen door. She ran.

Lillian and Allie took their place, hiding in a large bush beside the ramp of the porch. They were still and silent. Sounds of running feet and a door bursting open made the girls jump and hold their breath. Then as quickly as it started the running stopped.

From the stable, Joe's eyes widened. Big P stood beside the old stone well which was about halfway between the duck shelter and the farmhouse. Izzie was before him. In an instant, Big P pushed Izzie into the well. "Nooooooooooooo!" cried Joe. Big P was startled and looked toward the farmhouse. At the same time Joe yelled, Heather, standing on the porch saw what happened to Izzie and screamed, only louder. Big P ran after Heather as she raced toward the van. Heather got to the van and frantically tried to open the door. Her hands slipped several times as the van was still wet from all the rain. Big P was closing in.

Joe ran out of the stable toward the well. Joe's feet ran faster than she ever had before. When she got to the well she looked in and screamed down the well. "Izzie!"

"Help!" Izzie just screamed between gargles of water. Her arms reaching and grabbing at the wet slimy walls of the well. Her legs were heavy and weighing her down. She knew how to swim a little but this was different and she was aware of the danger she was in. The water tasted salty and she spit out every mouthful that got in her mouth from the splashing as she tried to scream for help. She was sinking and losing her battle to stay above the water. There was no sense of relief for Izzie, even though she could hear Joe. Joe grabbed the rope used for the well bucket and quickly fashioned a device using her superb mechanical skills for Izzie to grab on to.

Heather tried starting the old van. The engine turned over once... nothing. Then it started. She stepped hard on the gas after shifting into reverse but in all the mud, the rear wheels just spun. The van didn't move. Heather looked back to try again but the van was just sinking further in the mud. When she looked forward again, Big P was standing right in front of the van. He was soaked to the bone, breathing heavily and with such evil in his eyes, that Heather barely recognized him. Heather locked her door and reached over to lock the passenger door but it was already locked. In the rear view mirror she noticed that the rear doors weren't just unlocked, they were open. When she glanced forward again, Big P was gone.

"Izzie, grab a hold!" Joe dropped the rope down. Joe attached a metal grate that was used earlier for the barbeque. This would make it easy for Izzie to grab on to and help speed up the lowering of the rope because the cast iron grate was heavy. "Izzie grab the grate!" There was nothing. Joe heard the metal grate splash into the well water. She couldn't see Izzie or the water. The rope just disappeared into the dark depths of the now silent well. "Izzie!" she cried. There was nothing.

CHAPTER IX

All's not well that ends with a well...

JOE STOOD STARING INTO THE depth of the well. She screamed and screamed for Izzie to reply. The rope was wrapped around the spindle on the top of the well. She cranked the large wooden handle to raise the rope out of the water. She struggled to turn the crank. The tension on the rope was intense. Joe was strong and looked to see if maybe the rope was caught or twisted in the crank. Izzie was running out of time. Joe cranked harder and looked down into the well.

Where the darkness met light and the rope disappeared, there was a tiny strong hand holding the rope. Izzie gripped the metal grate with one hand and the rope with the other and used all her strength. She took a deep breath of air, something most people take for granted. Izzie knew that she may end up in the water again if Joe couldn't hold the crank. Joe cranked as hard as she could. Izzie broke through the darkness of the well bottom, still with a look of terror on her face. Izzie was alive but Joe's strength was running out. Izzie stopped going up and quickly realized that there was no way Joe was going to be able to crank the rope any higher with a soaking wet Izzie clamped on to it. Joe's hands started to slip and Izzie braced herself for the plunge. Nothing happened.

A second set of hands grabbed the crank with Joe. It was Allie. Allie strained with Joe and begged Izzie to hold on. Each turn was a test of their strength, their will, their friendship. With a final crank Izzie took one hand off the rope and grasped onto the rock wall of the well. Her elbow formed a ninety degree angle and the leverage she needed to get her other hand on the top of the rocky edge and pull herself out. She flopped into the mud, breathing heavily and in shock. Allie and Joe fell down next to Izzie breathing heavily and limp with exhaustion.

"Hey Allie."

"Ya Izzie?"

"I lost your ribbons. One's in the well. You want me to go back and get it?"

Allie briefly laughed. "Shopping. We will do lots of shopping when this is done."

"Let's go," Izzie ordered. She could see the Camp Candle Lake van. "Help me up."

"What about…" Allie started.

"Just leave it. There isn't time," Izzie commanded. Allie and Joe helped Izzie up and helped her toward the van.

In the farmhouse, Lillian sat in the kitchen where Allie had left her before racing to help Joe. She sat in a dark corner. She felt her way around the phone key pad that Allie had handed her. She dialled 9-1-1. There were footsteps on the porch. She hung up before the call could connect. She remained silent. From the kitchen where Lillian was you could hear the sound of the front door open. Then footsteps approaching. They stopped. Lillian didn't breathe. The room filled with the stench of Big P. There were keys jingling. The footstep sounds seemed to be moving further away.

Lillian took a breath, put her hand on the floor of the kitchen and shifted her body a little. Her hand was on a ribbon that was on the kitchen floor. She raised it to her nose to smell it. It was one of the two ribbons that Izzie had placed in her hair earlier that morning, a blue one that Allie had given her. Lillian held her breath. Lillian seemed uncharacteristically confused. As the footstep sounds moved seemingly a safe distance from Lillian, she called 9-1-1 again.

Back in the van, Heather froze. Big P wasn't there. She sat still, her hands still gripping the steering wheel. The engine seemed to quiet as she was not trying to move the van in the mud any longer. Her head did not move but her eyes danced around looking for Big P. The open rear doors screeched wide open and Heather screamed. Allie and Joe lifted Izzie by the arms into the back of the van. Heather looked shocked it was the girls.

Seeing Heather was instant relief for Izzie. The relief was short lived. Izzie heard a tractor and it was getting louder. Big P was driving the tractor directly toward the van. It had a large fork lift on the front that was used to move large stacks of hay, but those large metal spikes were now aimed to pierce right through the front of the van.

There was a huge crash as the tractor impaled the front of the van. Heather looked back and said "Girls get out." Allie and Joe were already gone. Izzie was starting to get back to her normal brilliant self. She was lying on her tummy and told Heather to get in the back. Heather did what she was told to do. Through the window they could see Big P driving the tractor. He was smiling an evil smile. Izzie could feel the tractor start to lift the van off the ground as Heather moved to the back.

As Big P smiled raising the van off the ground he felt a sudden jolt of mud hit his face from the left, then the right. Then more mud, and more. He stopped driving to wipe the mud from his face. It was thick and heavy. When he composed himself he looked and to his surprise he saw a tween throwing mud at him. It was Joe. Then he got hit again from the other side where Allie was. This complicated things greatly for Perdas. There were two kids there and they were throwing mud at him.

When the girls were in the back of the van, Allie motioned frantically that they had to stop him. It was Izzie who quickly devised a plan that they had to go on opposite sides of the tractor so that he couldn't chase them both at the same time. She was right. This complication seemed to frustrate Perdas and make him stop for the moment.

He wiped the mud from his face just to have more thrown at him. When he stood up, the emergency switch the tractor was equipped with, instantly shut down the motor. "Stop it!" yelled Big P. He looked at Joe, then over at Allie, each ready with another round of mud ammunition. The van creaked. Heather stood up and moved to the front of the van and looked out the window. The windshield was clouded and Heather used her sleeve to wipe it clear so she could see what was going on. Big P looked directly at Heather, then Joe, then

Allie. He continued to wipe the mud from his eyes, slowly and with purpose.

"Did it work?" Izzie asked as she laid in the back of the van.

"Well, he looks confused and muddy," Heather replied.

"You're not going to win!" he said. "So just stop." It was silent for a moment.

"No, you're not going to win," a voice shouted from the porch, "I've already called the police." To Big P's shock there was another tween standing on his front porch behind him.

In a fit of rage he went to run off the tractor. There are several places that you should not run, church, near a pool, and off a tractor. Big P slipped off the tractor, knocked his head on the metal side and laid face first in the mud. Thank goodness for safety switches and that the tractor was no longer moving, as his head was right in front of the tire. Instead of jail, it would have been the hospital for Big P. Izzie told the girls how to tie him up using the bungie cords in the back of the van.

Big P was fastened to the tractor and the girls sat in the back of the van with their legs hanging over the bumper staring down the long driveway anticipating help to arrive at any moment. Izzie reflected on the events of the day and tears started running down her cheeks. She was terrified, sad, happy and anxious all at the same time. Later, doctors would tell her that she was in shock from the events of the day. Heather put her arm around her and started to sing a soothing camp song. The girls of Cabin 29 just stared down the driveway quietly listening to Heather's comforting voice. Big P laid motionless, secured to the tractor, deep in mud. A pig came and started licking Big P's face.

CHAPTER X

Who bought the farm...

As Big P moaned and tried to move his face away from the piggy who kept at him like he was tasty lollipop, a truck pulled into the farm followed by the police. The sun was starting to peek through the clouds and a gentle breeze and warmth replaced the rains that just poured down. The truck came to a sudden stop and out came Vern and Fred. They ran to the girls. Vern took a two-way radio from his belt holster and radioed Camp Candle Lake that they had found the girls. Heather sat on the back of the van floor with her arms around Joe and Lillian. Allie and Izzie were now sitting on opposite sides of the van and leaned in toward the middle to stay warm under the blankets.

Vern walked up to the well where he saw Izzie's wheelchair. He picked it up and gave the wheels a spin to make sure it was in proper working order and brought it back to Izzie. Fred helped Izzie back into her familiar chair. There was a strange sense of familiarity and comfort for Izzie as she sat back and put her hands on the wheels.

"Guess I'm going to have to buy a new van," Fred said scratching his head and assessing what had happened. The tractor still held the van about six inches in the air by the large metal forks that pierced it. The van, like the blankets inside it, needed to be retired.

Heather went to apologize to Fred. "This is all my fault for losing Izzie in the first place."

"Heather, I've known you since you were a little camper and I know that you are not to blame." he reassured her. He pointed to the police taking Big P away in handcuffs.

Vern stopped Perdas on the way to the police cruiser. The police officer who held Big P by the handcuffs stopped and allowed Vern to speak to him.

"They're kids," Vern said in Perdas' face, "How could you do something like this?"

"It's about the money," said Izzie who wheeled up next to them on the stone path. "He was going to scare all Fred's…"

"Frank's!" interrupted Fred.

"…Fred's campers away. Then he was going to offer Fred a low price for the land so he could expand his farm," Izzie continued, "The expansion plans are all on his kitchen table along with the next batch of creepy letters he was going to give to the campers."

Lillian listening chimed in, "I suspect that he came up with the idea long before we got to camp. It would have been easy to scope out the cabins and know the routines as he was at the camp practically every day delivering food."

"And with the extra land he would be able to become a mega-farm, instead of a family farm," said Allie.

"Farms feed cities," said Joe

"But not small farms. Small farms feed camps and towns people. The real money is in feeding cities," Izzie finished.

"You know what else farms feed?" asked Vern to Big P

"What?" said Big P.

"Jails," said Vern and he gave him a little push as the officer took him away.

"Frank, we're going to need the kids for statements, is that okay?" asked an officer.

"Sure. Sure. Justine and I will call their parents and get these kids home as quickly as possible."

"What!?" exclaimed Izzie.

"I'm sure that you kids want to get home."

"Not a chance!" said Joe.

"If we go home, then Big P wins. It is exactly what he wanted. I will not let that man have any power over me. Fred… Frank, we want to stay," Lillian pleaded.

"Okay. Let's call your parents and we'll see what they say." He smiled.

"You girls are the bravest girls in the world. I am so proud of you," said Heather as she hugged Joe and Allie. "You are what makes Camp Candle Lake so great."

"We are the cabin that makes, cabin friends so great. We are the cabin that makes, cabin friends so great."

Izzie started the cheer and everyone, including Vern, joined in.

Back at the camp, after phone calls and visits from parents, things started to return back to normal camp life. By now, the heroics of the girl's actions had spread throughout the camp. Press and media agencies tried to get photos and interviews.

The girl's parents limited this, but the story went viral and Camp Candle Lake became incredibly popular. Calls and emails poured in from people wanting to sign up for the following summer. This would mean that even more people would have to be hired to care for, watch over, plan for, and feed the abundance of campers. Although tragic that it happened, the events that took place at the farm lead to the survival and success of Camp Candle Lake.

"In a way, the girls really saved this camp," said the slick banker.

"You could say that," replied Fred. "Here are your papers back."

Jason looked at them. "They aren't signed Frank."

"Nope. I'm not going to need the bank's money after all. Campers are happy, the registration is full for next year. We'll be fine without the bank's help. Sorry Jason." He patted him on the back and without even looking at him left to head to the mess hall. Jason stood there flabbergasted. It wasn't often he was turned down. Usually he was the one in power. This unfamiliar feeling left Jason standing, staring, and saying quietly under his breath, "But, but, but, but, but, but... the money I was going to make." Then he shouted as he got an idea; a clever money making banker idea.

"Wait!"

Fred stopped and turned around. "Jason, I don't need the money anymore."

"I know. I know. But you could use the land." Fred tilted his head in wonder. "Think Frank. You can expand the camp. You could accommodate all those new campers that are hitting your website and calling."

Fred thought out loud, "Think of the campers growing their own food. Think of the campers learning about local sustainable farming. Think of the campers learning about caring for animals."

"Think of the money," the banker said. Fred didn't seem impressed. "I mean, yes the children, campers, living in harmony with the planet. All good. All good." Jason recovered from his greedy side when he saw that it did not impress Fred at all.

"Let me think about it."

"Will do Frank, but I know that we could get that land for a song." Jason paused. "Funny."

"What's funny?" asked Fred.

"Perdas' plan may end up completely backfiring. You may end up with his land cheap instead of him getting yours."

"Either way, you make money though, right Jason?"

Jason smiled and pointed his finger of his right hand at Fred and with his left he took the rim of his sunglasses, pulled them down to the bridge of his nose, winked, and said, "Talk soon, Frank." He turned on the heel of his fancy shoes and made his way to the exit.

Fred continued down the path to the mess hall. He had lots to think about.

In the mess hall, things were pretty much back to normal. Mrs. Mendax seemed really on edge, but given the circumstances that took place just a few days ago, it was to be expected. Eliot and Lucas were sitting with Cabin 29. Cabin 29 pretty much got whatever they asked for since the events at the farm took place. They were heroines to the campers and so humble and respectful, it was pretty hard for Heather or any of the other counsellors to say no to them. The boys were laughing when Fred came by the table.

"What's so funny boys?" asked Fred with excitement.

"Hey Fred, does February march?" asked Lucas.

"No, but April may," jumped in Eliot.

Fred laughed as if he had never heard it before. "Good one boys. Where did you hear that one?"

"Last night we read a ton of them on this app called…" Eliot froze as Lucas hit his arm. "I mean. Um. Ugh."

"Boys, give the tablet to Justine in my office. You can have it back on your way home."

"Yes sir," they said sheepishly.

"Nice going," said Lucas under his breath to Eliot.

"Girls, enjoy your dinner." Fred said.

"Thank you," they all replied as if they were a chorus of school children greeting a teacher.

Heather came back to the table with a tray of food.

"What's with Mrs. Mendax? She's jumpy," Heather noted.

"Maybe it's because she was so close to Perdas." answered Izzie.

"Close?" asked Lillian.

"Yes. I saw them together every time I came up the ramp to get in the side door."

"You don't think she knew do you?" Allie asked leaning across the table in her awkwardly loud whisper.

"No way!" said Eliot.

"Guys! You can't jump to conclusions. She works here. She's the cook. The cook talks to the farmer. It is the way life goes," Lucas said trying to settle suspicions.

"Ya. I just want this to be over," said Joe.

"Me too," added Heather, "Now dig in."

Lillian took her plate and smelled deeply. Izzie looked at her plate, then at Allie. Allie looked at her plate and then at Lillian. Joe looked at her plate and plunged her fork into the casserole and started to inhale it as if she had never eaten before. No immediate harm came to Joe so the girls shrugged off suspicions that the food may be poisoned and dug in. Eliot just looked at the girls and smirked as he took his first bite. Then he coughed. He grabbed his throat and sunk to the floor from his chair. He gasped.

"What's going on?" asked Lillian.

"Oh my gosh, Eliot's been poisoned!" shouted Izzie.

CHAPTER XI

Camp is back to camp...

ELIOT BURST OUT LAUGHING. JOE kicked him from her chair as he laid next to her.

"It's not funny!" Joe said.

"Too soon," said Lucas. "Too soon." He shook his head in disapproval and smiled, then everyone laughed.

Camp went on for the rest of the summer, business as usual. Fred contacted a realtor to see about purchasing the farm and turn a negative into a positive. The kids went on canoe trips. They went on hikes. They played capture the flag and had regular campfires. Sessions went on like normal and Izzie became quite the marksman with the bow and arrow. Vern kept an eye on the kids a little closer and shared his plant growing experiments with Fred. Fred was so impressed with what Vern was doing that he offered Vern a piece of the newly acquired farmland to run his experiments and teach the campers his techniques. Vern told Fred that he was excited and looked forward to sharing his ideas with the young campers. Izzie already took an interest in it and Vern was teaching her and let her help him with his research.

On the last day at camp, Izzie pulled herself out of her wheelchair and into her lower bunk. She looked up at the bottom of the top bunk. Allie, Joe, and Lillian knelt down next to Izzie's bed.

"What's up?" she asked.

"Here, this is for you." Joe handed Izzie a marker.

"Sign it," said Lillian.

"Really?" said Izzie.

"Of course," said Allie.

Izzie took the cap off the marker and signed her name next to the other girl's names. She dotted her 'i' with a little bow.

"I can't wait to go shopping!" Allie yelled. Izzie took her pillow and smacked her with it. A pillow fight broke out and the girls laughed and laughed. Joe won.

Time past and the campers found themselves heading for home as the summer drew to a close. When she got home, Izzie had nightmares a few times from the experience and spoke with doctors to learn to deal with it. She was tough and smart and knew that she needed help. She didn't even hesitate when her mom asked her if she wanted to go back to Camp Candle Lake the next summer. Little did she know that there was another mystery to solve.

Allie unpacked all of her camp outfits. She gave a lot of them away to charities knowing that she would outgrow them before the next time she went camping. Allie spoke to her mom about shopping the next spring for new outfits to take to camp. The camp would be even bigger and better. She had mini-celebrity status at the camp. Her and her friends were kind of treated like rock stars. Two weeks before camp, Allie checked her mailbox and got a letter.

Lillian unpacked all of her stuff. She put it all back exactly where it belonged in her room so she would easily find everything before the next time she went camping. Lillian already filled out the camp registration for next spring to send to the camp. The camp would be even bigger and better. She had mini-celebrity status at the camp. Her and her friends were kind of treated like rock stars. Two weeks before camp, Allie sent Lillian a voice message and told her to check her mailbox. She did and in it was a letter.

Joe left all of her stuff packed for weeks. She put it all exactly where it belonged in her room, on the floor. It would be so difficult to find what she needed before the next time she went camping. Joe already completed the meal plan suggestions to send to the camp for next spring. The camp would be even bigger and better. She had mini-celebrity status at the camp. Her and her friends were kind of treated like rock stars. Two weeks before camp, Allie sent Joe a text message and told her to check her mailbox. She did and in it was a letter.

Izzie unpacked all of her stuff. She put it all back exactly where it belonged, in a storage closet. She would leave it there until the next time she went camping. Izzie already looked forward to school in the fall but she was thinking about going to the camp. The camp would be even bigger and better but would it be safer? She did look forward to the mini-celebrity status her and her friends had at the camp. They were kind of treated like rock stars, and Izzie loved it. Two weeks before camp, Allie sent Izzie a text message and told her to check her mailbox. She did and in it was a letter.

All the girls from Cabin 29 got the same letter.

EPILOGUE

THE WHEELS KEEP ON TURNING...

Perdas sat in his jail cell. He reflected on what went wrong that day. When he sat down at a small table he began writing this...

J,

Our plan failed but it's not my fault. You need to know that I had no intention of hurting anyone but they forced me to. I thought for sure that with your inside information about the camp and my plan that we would be an unstoppable team. When that girl chased me into the woods, I figured that she knew it was me. She followed me half way to my farm until I lost her by the 'Bus Eater' rapids. I thought I would cool suspicions by making like the nice guy and offer a field trip to the farm. That seemed to be working too. When that little girl in the wheelchair showed up at my house I didn't see any harm in letting her in and using the washroom. After all, she's just a kid in a wheelchair. I went upstairs to get a new shirt as the one I was wearing smelled like smoke from the bonfire. I hate smoke. When I came down the little girl was in the kitchen. She saw the stuff on the kitchen table. I didn't know what to do. I grabbed her chair and wheeled her into a closet until I could think of what to do. Then when the storm hit, it was too easy; throw her in the well. I knew it would look like an accident and that no one noticed because of that storm. But those kids came back just as I was getting her in the well. I never saw the little ones, only Heather. When Heather got the van stuck in the mud I actually laughed. I went back in the house to get the keys. Had I known there was a kid in there calling the cops, believe me, I would have dealt with that first. But I thought it was too perfect. I went to the tractor and was just going to dump the van in the pond with Heather in it and make it look like it was an accident from the storm. I could've then taken the girl out of the well and put her in the pond too. It would have been easy to tell the police that the kid was left behind when the storm hit and after Heather had picked her up that they drove off the road and into the pond. No one would have suspected us as I had no reason or motive for hurting a little girl and no one knows about you, yet. This would also helped our plan move faster by sending fear into the hearts of the other campers. Like we planned, the camp would've closed and force Frank to sell us the land. Now things are even more complicated. You need to sell my land and use the money to get me a good lawyer. No one knows we're working together. You need to get those girls. You need to get Fred. You need to get me out of here. If you don't...everyone will know we're working together because I'll tell the cops you're working with me. When you get this letter, burn it.

    P.

J,

Our plan failed but it's not my fault. You need to know that I had no intention of hurting anyone but they forced me to. I thought for sure that with your inside information about the camp and my plan that we would be an unstoppable team. When that girl chased me into the woods, I figured that she knew it was me. She followed me halfway to my farm until I lost her by the BusEater rapids. I thought I would cool suspicions by making like the nice guy and offer a field trip to the farm. That seemed to be working too. When that little girl in the wheelchair showed up at my house I didn't see any harm in letting her in and using the washroom. After all, she's just a kid in a wheelchair. She came in the front door off the ramp that I had made when mamma was in her wheelchair.

I went upstairs to get a new shirt as the one I was wearing smelled like smoke from the bonfire. I hate smoke. When I came down the little girl was in the kitchen. She saw the stuff on the kitchen table. I didn't know what to do. I grabbed her chair and wheeled her into a closet until I could think of what to do. Then when the storm hit, it was too easy; throw her in the well. I knew it would look like an accident and that no one noticed because of that storm. But those kids came back just as I was getting her in the well. I never saw the little ones; only Heather. When Heather got the van stuck in the mud I actually laughed.

I went back in the house to get the keys. Had I known there was a kid in there calling the cops, believe me, I would have dealt with that first. But I thought it was too perfect. I went to the tractor and was just going to dump the van in the pond with Heather in it and make it look like it was an accident from the storm. I could've then taken the girl out of the well and put her in the pond too. It would have been easy to tell the police that the kid was left behind when the storm hit and after Heather had picked her up that they drove off the road and into the pond. No one would have suspected us as I had no reason, or motive for hurting a little girl. This would also helped our plan move faster by sending fear into the hearts of the other campers. Like we planned, the camp would've closed and force Frank to sell us the land. Now things are even more complicated. You need to sell my land and use the money to get me a good lawyer. No one knows we're working together. You need to get Fred. You need to get me those girls. You need to get me out of here. If you don't.... everyone will know we are working together because I'll tell the cops you're working with me.

When you get this letter, burn it.

P.

CPSIA information can be obtained
at www.ICGtesting.com
Printed in the USA
LVOW13s1520151116

513060LV00008B/681/P